The Year that Trembled

For Tom —
In peace
and friendship
& the CULT! —

# The Year that Trembled

### A NOVEL

**Scott Lax**

Paul S. Eriksson, *Publisher*
Forest Dale, Vermont

Library of Congress Cataloging-in-Publication Data


Lax, Scott.
    The year that trembled : a novel / Scott Lax.
        p.    cm.
    ISBN 0-8397-8660-3 (hardcover)
    1. Vietnamese Conflict. 1961-1975—Ohio—Fiction.  I. Title
PS3562.A962443    1998                                      98-21845
813'.54—dc21                                                    CIP

Design by Eugenie S. Delaney

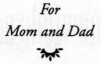

*For*
*Mom and Dad*

# Acknowledgments

My gratitude to The Bread Loaf Writers' Conference, and in particular the following teachers and friends: Michael Collier, Gerard Donovan, Amy Hempel, Ron Hansen, Ann Hood, Carol Knauss, Helen Schulman, Kristen Lindquist, Sebastian Matthews, Robert Pack, Tom Perotta and Frances Richards. Special thanks go to Richard Hawley, for his inspiration, and Ron Powers, for his enduring advice and encouragement during the writing of this book.

For their moral support and help, my appreciation to: Fanfan Anento, Traci Bryant, David Budin, Jay Craven, Peggy and Paul Eriksson, Tim Hagan, Catherine Kilbane, Liz Ludlow, Mike Mayor, Trisha O'Brien, Peter Waters and Kristen Worley.

For their help with my research, I am grateful to Cleveland's *Scene Entertainment Weekly* and The United States Selective Service System.

My deepest thanks to my family — My nephews Jamie and Tyler Davidson, my sister Pat Davidson, and my parents, Josephine and Milton J. Lax.

And thanks to John Paxton Osborne, in memoriam.

Year that trembled and reel'd beneath me!
Your summer wind was warm enough,
    yet the air I breathed froze me,
A thick gloom fell through the sunshine and darken'd me,
Must I change my triumphant songs? said I to myself,
Must I indeed learn to chant the cold dirges of the baffled?
And sullen hymns of defeat?

— WALT WHITMAN
     From the poem, "Year That
     Trembled and Reel'd Beneath Me,"
     Book XXL, "Drum Taps,"
     from *Leaves of Grass*

# 1.

# Meadow

꼭

I lived beside a meadow.

The farmhouse I lived in and the meadows and woodlands that surrounded it were first called Little Meadow by the family that settled on the lush north bank of northeastern Ohio's Shaguin River. The settlers had built their house and barn in the late 1850s, turning Little Meadow into a small, working farm. The barn had been torn down and carted away years ago, but the house remained largely unchanged for more than a hundred years.

Sometime during the passing of the last few generations before I moved in, Little Meadow had again become what it had once replaced — a meadow. With the crops and domestic animals gone, the meadows that bordered the house on three sides filled in with wildflowers and grasses. The various owners maintained the meadow, burning or mowing it periodically to keep out maturing shrubs and trees. There were no farm animals left; rabbits, deer, fox, squirrels, skunks and raccoons roamed the meadows and woods that bordered the south meadow all the way down to the Shaguin — an American Indian word meaning "clear water" — a hundred yards away.

When dusk fell on Little Meadow, when the blue spruce and white pine trees that formed its boundaries became shadows, as the sun that had set over those first settlers faded and vanished, as the bull frogs from the small pond fifty feet to the east of the house sang their ancient mating songs, that family must have felt a kind of peacefulness. During the time that I lived there as a young man, despite everything that was to happen, I often felt that peace.

One early mid-September evening in 1970 the golden, horizontal sunlight washed over Little Meadow, washed over all of us who lived in the white, two story farmhouse: Jeff Robins, Phil Rosenbaum, Jim "Hairball" Morton and me, all of us recent graduates of Chestnut Falls High School.

We moved to Little Meadow early that summer. There we found a beautiful place, one that none of us knew existed within the limits of our small town until I read an ad in the *Chestnut Valley Herald* for four rooms to rent in an old farmhouse. The north meadow where we stood that night had filled in with grasses and plants that had bloomed and faded through the summer. Some of the plants, the goldenrods and swamp milkweed, still held their flowers even as fall approached. Throughout the growing season the meadow was alive with the changing colors of its inhabitants: fireweed, rough blazing star, lupine, bluebell, wild white indigo, switchgrass, bachelor's button, pimpernel, Joe-pye weed, prickly poppy, fawn lily. That night, everything in the meadow — the six of us, as well as the grasses, plants, flowers and trees — was covered in the brief, flattening light of early fall.

Our neighbors, Charlie and Helen Kerrigan, stood with us in the meadow. They lived on the east end of Little Meadow in a cracked and faded English Tudor house. Charlie was three years older than we, and he, too, had gone to Chestnut Falls High School. Helen was an import from the east, from Connecticut, an artist who had come to town for an education at the Cleveland Institute of Art. Instead she found her lanky, brooding husband-to-be. Helen postponed her dreams to be with Charlie.

The four of us and Charlie and Helen had moved into the rental houses in June, our leases consisting of handshakes with Catherine Smith, a petite, red-haired English teacher from our old high school.

I close my eyes now and can see Charlie's face, and Helen's, most clearly. Charlie looked at Helen as she talked about the sun. The colors of the sunset, she said, were the most wonderful of any in the day. Sunsets, Helen said, were the sun's way of making everything it lit become beautiful, so that the animals and the plants of the world would love it and so welcome it back the next morning. The sun, she told us, needed to be loved. That was why it existed.

None of us laughed at Helen. Maybe because in 1970 we listened more to new ideas, however sentimental or foolish they sound all these years later in the harsh light of the millennium's end. We wanted to find new answers for old questions, or we just thought there were new answers. And even with all the death that came daily, the death that would come to our gathering in the meadow, life in America felt as if it were being recast, reshaped, even redeemed by some transcendent thing.

What the thing was we debated long and loud: God, Jesus, Buddha, Krishna, the perfect meditative self. Or drugs, for some. Or those things which fueled the passions of so many bewildered wartime youth: the idea of peace; our music; love in all its base and sublime forms.

Music, rebellious, romantic, filled with anger and anesthetic, nourished us in the days when a boy might find himself standing, not in a meadow, but in a burning jungle in Southeast Asia, the memory of high school graduation as recent as the ending of the baseball season.

Music had the power to take a grain off of the mountain of pain that was the burden of surviving someone's untimely death. Our songs cushioned our fall from grace, threw us a life-line as we dove like rats from a sinking ship into the boiling sea of war and commerce.

The fortunate ones found meaning in love. At that moment of dusk, Charlie Kerrigan looked at his young wife, Helen, the setting sun turning her face the color of the marigolds that dotted the flower beds at our farmhouse, as if she was Truth itself. As the meadow quieted down and the light moved west across the earth, Charlie seemed to rise up out of himself with his love for Helen. She spoke about the sun and the sky, about what she wished for: that we would be safe in the months to come; that the country would be at peace. We listened without interruption. Her words seemed to suspend momentarily in the air, then float down like blossoms from a cottonwood tree in June. When she finished, the usually reserved Charlie kissed her in front of us — four awed and yearning boys.

Jeff would later say, with the unexpected tenderness that young men, momentarily shaken from witnessing expressions of love, exhibit so rarely and lose so soon, that it was as if the light came from heaven and settled on Helen and Charlie.

The wind blew gently and the grasses made harmonic counterpoint with the wind and the ground seemed to breathe, as if it would swallow Charlie and Helen, or blow them away, or move them down the river like two sailboats. Helen was twenty-one years old and lovely. She had dark brown eyes and long brown hair streaked with a few strands of silver. An ageless beauty, she flowed over us, a cold stream over jagged rocks.

Charlie and Helen said goodnight. They turned and walked slowly to their house, the fading flowers and smooth grass of the meadow parting for them like a miniature sea — not Moses's great sea, parted by faith, but a personal sea, just large enough to hold the two of them.

No airplanes or cars or barking dogs interrupted the brushing sound of the flowers and grass against their legs, a sound I imagined heard as long as people had loved each other, as long as lovers moved away from the setting sun, away from conversation, society and well-meaning friends, if only for the night, if only to be together long enough to shield each other from everything but their own attempt to love.

Jeff, Hairball, Phil and I waited until the sunset that streaked the sky pink and orange and purple disappeared and the stars came out.

Hairball lay on his back and smoked one cigarette after another. He'd light the match and hold it until it nearly burned his fingers, then in a clean motion, light the cigarette, shake the match once, and put it in the pocket of his jeans. Littering was a venal sin to Hairball, worthy of his considerable rage. He used the front of his old jeans as an ashtray. When he'd finish his cigarette, he'd crush it out with his fingers and stuff it into the same right front pocket where his match had gone. Jeff once had called him "the human ashtray." Hairball threw his lit cigarette at Jeff's crotch. A bitter argument followed with no resolution, but the victory was quietly Hairball's: Jeff never made the reference again.

Phil, short and compact, closed his eyes and hummed an original song. He wanted to be a rock star and he made the effort to look the part. On his head sat a mountain of hair that he called his Jew-fro. The Jewfro was — like the skin-tight black jeans, snakeskin cow-boy boots, red suede pouch dangling from a macrame belt, and red and black form-fitting cowboy shirt — his rock and roll calling card.

Jeff looked as if he accidentally got separated from the rest of Jesus's disciples. His hazel eyes glowed with the youthful spiritual-ity that came from his searching heart. I imagined him dressed in a white robe and sandals rather in the baggy plaid bermuda shorts, red hi-top sneakers, black socks and tight white tee shirt that he lived in during warm weather.

He moved his gangly body toward a white pine tree, flicked the sandy brown hair that fell perpetually into his eyes, and broke off some boughs as an offering to the Buddhist altar in his bedroom.

Hairball watched him suspiciously. "Superstition," he said as Jeff loped back toward the rest of us.

"It's an offering to my Buddha nature, dumbass," Jeff replied seriously, flicking his hair and waving the pine. "You should try it, Hairball. You could chant for a new job. Or a girlfriend. Or to get out of the draft . . . like me."

Jeff brightened and ran awkwardly at Hairball and slapped him across the back of his head with the handful of white pine.

"Time for you to die," Hairball said in his gravel voice, grabbing the weaker Jeff and slamming him to the ground with a wrestling hold. Jeff, who loathed fighting, groaned.

"God *dammit*, Hairball. Let me up. Let me *up*, god *dammit!*"

Hairball wedged his arm across Jeff's neck and grunted hap-pily. "Call me the Buddha first. Say I'm the Buddha."

"Don't. Get off," Jeff cried, swinging wildly at the air.

"Get off him, Hairball," I said. Phil and I laughed. "Give the guy a break."

"Call me Buddha, Jeffey," Hairball hissed.

"You can sit on me all night and I'll never call you Buddha," Jeff said, his voice strained. You're gonna get *botsu* for this."

"I'm gonna get what?" Hairball said, laughing hoarsely.

"*Botsu* — Buddhist punishment," Jeff said. "Bad effects for your bad causes."

Suddenly Hairball, breathing heavily, rolled off of Jeff onto his back and took out a cigarette. "*Botsu*," he said, pondering the new idea. "*Botsu*. Whatever. You go chant, Jeff. And while you're at it, chant for me to get out of the draft. Me no want to die, Buddha Man. That'd be cool, bro."

"Huh," Jeff replied, the sound a cross between a shout and a sob. He stood up and brushed the grass off his plaid bermudas. "I'll chant for you not to be such a doofus, how's that?"

Hairball, by now content again, lit a match, watched it burn down, lit the cigarette, shook the match, and blew the smoke out first through his nose, then his mouth. He put the match in his pocket, his face glistening with sweat. "That's better than a sharp stick in the ass," he said dreamily.

The sun had taken with it the warmth and the cool night breezes began to blow from the northwest. We walked back to the farmhouse to do what we usually did on weeknights: Phil to his music; Hairball to his beer and tequila and pot; Jeff to his chanting and Buddhist study; and me to nothing much — television, records, or back outside to walk around with my dog, Lion.

Instead of going to our rooms, though, we drifted into the

kitchen and sat around the white metal table. I lit the olive colored gas stove and put on a pot of water for tea. Hairball fished around in the drawer for a bottle opener for the beer. Phil went into the living room and put "Helplessly Hoping" by Crosby, Stills and Nash on the record player.

"Excellent," Hairball yelled. "This song is excellent."

Hairball surveyed his three housemates with a blissful smile.

Halfway through the song, Hairball's smile left his face. Phil sighed and said, "So, anyway, you guys. What. Nice night."

Then Hairball opened up the moment with the one topic that was never far from our minds.

"I'll tell you what. I'll tell you what right now. The draft lottery's going to get one of us," he said in an low, almost inaudible voice. "One of us is going to that hell-hole before it's over. I'm sure of it. Damn sure."

No one moved, as if we were waiting out a buzzing bee.

"Well," Phil said at last, "it's not gonna be me." His mouth turned up, his eyes didn't smile. "I'll wear black lace panties and tell them Army boys that I'm a homo." His smile faded. "I'm not going. No way. And you know what else by the way? Screw Nixon, screw Nam, and screw you for being so depressing, Hairball."

Hairball laughed. The phlegmy, croup-like explosion sent Lion running out the kitchen screen door in a black blur.

"You do that, Phil. But somebody's going. I'm telling you. Law of averages. One of us is going."

I said, "I think it might be me."

They were quiet for a few seconds.

"What'll you do then, man?" Hairball asked.

"Do? Meaning?" I said.

"What-will-you-do-if-you-get-draf-ted-Case-y? What the hell do you think I mean?" said Hairball, coughing hard and reaching for another Stroh's.

"I don't know. Try for a conscientious objector, maybe. Or I'll go to Canada. Hell, maybe I'll even go to Nam."

I didn't know why I said that. Was it true? It was the first time I'd considered it.

Hairball slammed his fist down on the metal table. "How could you go, man? You'd be a hypocrite if you went, Casey. You'd be a chicken-shit if you went. That's the stupidest thing I've ever heard you say and I've heard you say some stupid things."

"There's a switch, anyway," said Phil.

"Meaning what?" said Hairball.

"Well for chrissake, Hairball," Phil said. "People say a guy's a chicken-shit if he doesn't go to Nam. Now you're saying Casey's a chicken-shit if he does go, if he doesn't dodge the draft."

"Look here, bro." Hairball cracked a Stroh's and pounded half the bottle down, finishing up with a big "ahhh." He lowered his head and fixed his watery blue eyes on Phil. "He raised hell for the last two years of school." He looked at me and smiled. "My man Casey here almost got us kicked out of school when he called a strike on Motory Day."

"Motory Day?" Jeff mouthed at me.

"Moratorium Day, Hairball. But go on," Phil said.

"Like I said, he got us to write poems and shit in his underground newspaper, okay? He was Mr. Protester. He can't go to Nam. Everything he said would be a lie."

Hairball turned to look at me. "You should go to jail before you go to Nam, Casey. Or at least Canada." He was serious.

I knew he was right. At least I had known what he said was right, back in school, back when I had answers and the issue seemed so simple. But now that the draft was so close my options seemed to be a jumble of bad choices.

"All I'm saying is that I don't know what I'd do. I'm trying to be honest, I guess. Anyway, I think I'm getting drafted. I don't know why. I just do."

"Well, that would make sense, in a way. Cosmic retribution and all that," said Phil.

"Cosmic what? What the hell are you talking about, Phil?" Hairball asked, coughing again. He took a long drink of Stroh's.

"You mean karmic," said Jeff. "You mean karmic retribution."

"Cosmic, karmic — damn, boy, what difference does it make?"

"It makes a difference. Cosmic doesn't mean anything. Karmic means that Casey's going to get his effect, good or bad, for the cause he made to stop the war. Or, check this out: the cause he made to keep it going — 'Aid and comfort to the enemy.' There's that argument."

"So which will it be, Buddha Man?" Hairball said. "Will Casey get drafted or not?"

"It will be," Jeff said, pausing dramatically. "It will be whatever it will be. There's no way to know until it happens."

Phil waited until the Crosby, Stills and Nash record finished playing and put on Marvin Gaye and Tammi Terrell.

"My main man, Marvin," Phil said. "Marvin and Tammi got the real thing. *Ain't* nothing like the real thing baby. Ain't *nothing* like the real thing."

"Could you believe Charlie and Helen tonight? Speaking of the real thing," Jeff said. "Charlie's a new man, that's for sure."

"I love Helen," Hairball wistfully, then gave a grunt.

Phil said, "You love her. So what. We all love Helen, man. I'd marry her myself if she wasn't with Charlie. I mean, I'm happy for Charlie and all that. I am. But Helen's perfect. She's beautiful. You know who she reminds me of? Ali McGraw."

"No way, man," Jeff said. "Katherine Ross, but with darker hair. Yeah. Katherine Ross, like in 'The Graduate.'"

"You guys are nuts," Hairball said. "Helen's that girl in 'I Love You, Alice B. Toklas.' What's her name, Case?"

"Leigh Taylor-Young," I said.

Everybody laughed. Leigh Taylor-Young was the hippie sex-goddess of our dreams.

"Okay, okay. But I've got to say that Helen doesn't remind me of any of them. So how's this: Helen sets her own standard."

A short silence followed.

"Not bad," Phil said. "Really. Not bad, Casey."

"Helen sets her own standard," Hairball repeated, squinting his eyes at me and tapping the table with his beer bottle as he spoke each word. "Better than Leigh Taylor-Young. *Better* than Leigh Tay-lor-Young. Wow."

"Charlie's got good karma, man," Jeff said. "He found his true love early on."

"Why is that good karma?" Phil said. "He met her and fell in love. He didn't do anything. He just got lucky, Buddha Man. Lucky, lucky, lucky. Right, Hairball?"

Hairball leaned back on his chair, cradled his eighth or ninth Stroh's of the night, gave us all a big smile and said in his growl, "Damn straight, bro!" and then let out a cannon-like belch that woke Lion, who had come back inside, out of his kitchen floor nap. My dog slid frantically toward the back door, his toenails making skates out of his paws on the faded blue linoleum.

Hairball laughed, then Phil, then me, then Jeff, and we laughed until tears came to our eyes.

Phil wiped his eyes with the sleeve of his cowboy shirt, looked up and said, "Hairball. You are hopeless, man. You are one funny cat. I hope you don't get your big old blond hair ball shot off in Nam."

"Yeah, bro, you too. Don't get your . . . ." Hairball's voice drifted off.

We went on like that for a while longer — four eighteen-year-olds in a farmhouse by a meadow in Ohio in the autumn of 1970, not wanting the night to end, drinking tea and beer, laughing and arguing about love and karma and about who the war would take, as the breezes of late September chilled us for the first time that season. The draft lottery, three months away, hovered, a helicopter with a passenger list that no one would show us.

The crickets and cicadas outside, who would be gone within weeks, sounded like sleigh bells in the kitchen. Just after midnight Hairball poured the last half of a beer down his throat and said, "I'm crashing. You idiots keep it down now."

"I'm with Hairball," Phil said, slugging him in the arm as they walked by.

Jeff got up, washed out his tea cup, and said, "'Night, Casey. Don't let it get to you. It's only our whole generation that's getting screwed. We'll know soon enough anyway. Whatever it'll be. We'll know soon enough." He walked part of the way up the stairs, then stopped and turned around. "Hell, man, maybe it'll be me."

My housemates went off to their rooms. Soon the music of The

Grateful Dead, Hairball's favorite band, wafted out of his room, along with the smell of his latest stash of Thai stick. Phil listened to Jimi Hendrix and mourned the guitarist who had died of an overdose a week earlier. He grieved honestly, as if for a friend. Twice I'd heard him crying.

Jeff lit incense and began his evening *Gongyo* — his Buddhist prayers. The sound of his chanting, with the music from Hairball's and Phil's rooms, was like a glorious, mad choir of confused angels.


I poured myself another cup of tea and walked out on the front porch and sat with Lion. The air was crisp and the stars were spread across the sky and I could hear the trees and grass moving together, whispering. Ever since I was a child I couldn't look up at the stars for very long or I'd feel like I'd be drawn into them, so I talked to Lion, kept myself earthbound. A border collie mix, Lion had black satin fur and a small white star on his chest. He sat with his long snout on my thigh and when I talked to him he made little dog sighs through his nose. His ears followed the night sounds at Little Meadow. Instead of investigating as usual, he stayed with me, his tail wagging slowly, blinking his big brown eyes, sighing.

I fell asleep in the broken white wicker chair on the porch. I didn't dream, but I heard the trees and the grass moving together, and felt the breeze across my face, and the cold from the north began to move through my clothes, onto my skin, into me. Autumn came to Little Meadow that night. I knew what was happening around me as I slept; I saw and felt and heard those things and still I slept, not understanding why my senses were awake and my body asleep. When I woke up Lion was sleeping at my feet. The night was at its deepest and Little Meadow was gone from sight, from my sight.

# 2.

# Meeting

We sat on our knees and faced a large black altar with gold foil trim and a gold emblem of a crane on the front. A scroll with Chinese characters printed on it hung inside. Surrounding the altar were the same kinds of offerings I'd seen in Jeff's room: evergreens, fruit, candles, a small black lacquer incense holder. Thick green-gray smoke filled the Buddhist Community Center with the scent of sandalwood. Our hands held the Buddhist prayer beads that a smiling Japanese man had given us when we walked in. "They help you to chanting," he said. "You chanting now, okay?"

"I don't know what anybody's saying. What're they yelling at?" Hairball asked.

"They're chanting that chant that Jeff does every morning and night when he wakes us up. What we're supposed to be doing."

"It doesn't sound the same, Case."

He smelled of stale beer and cigarettes and couldn't sit still.

"It's the same chant but all these people say it so it sounds different, I guess."

"We're going to hell. It sounds satanic. I do not want to be doing no damn devil worship, bro."

"We're not going to hell. We're chanting to get out of the draft. Jeff says we can get anything we want, and that's what we want, right? Let's humor Jeff, anyway. He's been bugging us to come to one of these meetings since the beginning of summer."

Hairball leaned closer. His voice dropped in pitch to a growl. "That's not all you want, Case." He smiled his crooked smile.

Across the room, sitting near the front of the group with three Japanese women, was the object of Hairball's observation.

Her dark blond hair was parted in the middle and grew down to her narrow waist. She turned two or three times to her right to check out the room and enabled me to see a face that set off alarms all over my body. She had a heart-shaped mouth, clear gray eyes, long eyelashes and freckles. Her small breasts were covered by a thin, gauzy white blouse. She had sewn an orange and purple peace symbol on the right thigh of her bell-bottom jeans and wore a necklace of multicolored love beads. Her feet were bare.

I mouthed the words of the chant: *Nam-myoho-renge-kyo*, over and over again. You were supposed to think about what you wanted as you said them. I breathed too fast and felt dizzy.

"Hairball. I know what I want."

His massive lump of tangled yellow hair had drooped toward his left shoulder. I heard his labored breathing, the usual precursor to snoring, and gave his shoulder a shove.

"Hairball, wake up."

"Whathefugsup?" Hairball yelled, terrified at being awakened in this peculiar place. I grabbed him as he tried to jump up and I pulled him down. A young blond guy about our age turned around and smiled at Hairball, rubbed his prayer beads together and mouthed the words, "It's okay, just chant." He had almost 1950s style short hair. His dress, like that of the other boys, was conservative but odd: he wore a stained, powder blue tie, white shirt and white pants. His black nylon socks had holes in them, a kind of anti-hippie facsimile of adult wear, but with a religious twist.

Hairball shook his head to clear away an invisible mist and began chanting, although the sound that came out of his mouth was unintelligible, an infantile yammer. He seemed pleased at the sound of it, though, and his voice got louder by the second until he was in danger of drowning everyone out.

I thought what I'd said to him hadn't registered in his beery brain, but a minute or so later he leaned over to me.

"She's your dream girl, Casey boy. Go after her or I will."

All of us from Little Meadow had come with Jeff to the Buddhist meeting. Helen sat with Charlie in the back of the room, on the opposite side from Hairball and me. Phil sat in the middle, in a row of Japanese women. At the front of the room sat Jeff. Someone rang a bell and the chanting ended. An older black man who had led the chanting turned around and faced the people in the room. His outfit set him apart. He wore a short-sleeved, off-white, polyester shirt with a western-style bolo tie and black pants. "Good afternoon," he shouted. His face broke open into an ecstatic grin.

"Good afternoon, *Shibucho*!" the crowd shouted back in unison.

"Good afternoon who?" Hairball asked.

"Don't know," I said.

At once people began jumping to their feet and singing songs. The black man called out, "Young Men's Division." Jeff and twenty or so clean cut guys jumped up and led the room in a song that sounded like a Japanese melody with English words about world peace and being as fierce and courageous as lions. The guys looked grim, as if they had the weight of the world on their shoulders. They waved their arms in rhythm with the song in a fierce, samuri-like manner. Everybody sang along except the guests. Helen tried to follow the words, which were printed on a piece of blue paper. After the song the black man yelled out "Women's Division," and some older women, mostly Japanese, stood up and sang another equally unfamiliar tune, this one about moonlight smiling in the night and someone called Sensei. Then he shouted, "Men's Division," and five or six men stood up and led their tune, a Buddhist version of the song "Hava Nagilia" that substituted the refrain, "Have a *Gohonzon*," which it turned out was the name of the scroll in the box that everybody chanted to. They, of all the divisions, looked pretty miserable with their pot bellies and crew cuts and darting eyes. "These guys don't want to be here," I thought. The sight of them in their white clothes, singing a Jewish song about the scroll in the box and looking so conflicted made me kind of giddy. I knew the tune, so I followed the words on a sheet of orange paper held by the Japanese lady next to me. As I sang, she patted me on the back and laughed merrily.

"My name Yuki," the tiny woman sang out to me. "Yah! A ha ha ha ha ha!"

She was the happiest human being I'd ever seen, and I laughed along with her.

Then the leader said, "Young Women's Division," and about fifteen girls, ranging from ten years old to their late teens, stood up and sang "You Are My Sunshine." It was as if a force of nature had come in through the air vents. The young women all smiled, but unlike the young men, they seemed to be enjoying themselves instead of posturing. They wore big smiles that looked fairly genuine, if a little nuts, which I was used to in 1970. I had convinced myself that nuts, during a war, wasn't necessarily a bad thing.

I looked up at them and right away locked eyes with the girl with the orange and purple peace symbol on her jeans. "You are my sunshine/my only sunshine/You make me happy/When skies are gray" she sang, and her eyes never left mine. I could hear her voice cutting through the room, bright and clear.

The smell of soy sauce mingled with cigarette smoke and sandalwood incense. In the small smokey room just off the main chanting room a dozen or so Japanese ladies sat eating rice balls and drinking green tea. They laughed, smoked, ate and talked all at the same time and with amazing speed. As I watched them I heard a voice behind me.

"How happy do you want to be?"

I turned and saw her.

"Me? How happy?"

If she had been attractive from across the room she was devastating up close. Her perfume or body lotion reminded me of the jasmine at my grandmother's house in Florida. I could see the curve of her waist and the outline of her breasts through her thin shirt. I thought she must have been about my age, but her eyes shone with a confidence that had surely escaped my life so far.

"If you try chanting you can change your life. You can have anything you want. You can be happy."

"I'd like to be happy, I guess," I said. My face burned and I ran my hand through my hair.

She took my right hand in hers. "I'm Jennifer Treman. I can help you be happy."

"Like I said, I wouldn't mind being happy. Is that why you chant? To be happy? One of my roommates chants but I'm never sure why. He's a good guy, but I wouldn't exactly call him happy."

Jennifer stopped smiling. I didn't want to offend her, even if I had to lie about how morose Jeff could be.

"Of course, now that I think of it, he does seem more cheerful lately," I said. "Uh, huh. Much more cheerful. In a deep way, is that it? Happy but deep? Or spiritually happy, maybe, but outwardly serious? He seems spiritually happy. Definitely spiritually happy, at least in the sense that, you know, he's not running around laughing every minute, but you can tell he's happy deep down. Happy like that?" A sick feeling rose in my stomach. I'm a fool, I thought.

"Sort of. But there's much more. It all depends on what you want." She was as relaxed as I was tense.

"You look like you might need a glass of water or something. You want something? A rice ball, maybe?" Jennifer smiled and nodded toward a small room full of laughing Japanese women who were standing over a counter rolling rice and seaweed into small balls.

"Me? Do I? I'm cool. I'm fine. Thanks though."

The mid-day sun came in through a dirty window behind Jennifer and lit up her blond hair. The Japanese ladies watched us from the smoky room and giggled. Charlie, Helen and Jeff sat listening earnestly to the man who had led the chanting and called out the songs. Helen nodded every few seconds as the man gestured elegantly and spoke in a strong, low voice. Every now and then the little group would laugh knowingly at something he said.

"That's Jack Daniels. Talking to your friends. He's very enlight-ened."

"Jack Daniels. Like the whiskey. Enlightened?"

"Yes. Jack Daniels like the whiskey. But you don't need whiskey to be happy when you chant."

Charlie had introduced me to shots of Jack Daniel's with a Stroh's chaser at Whirly's, the bar downtown. All through the summer we'd meet at Whirly's after work and eat Ernie Whirly's famous Whirlyburger and drink beer. I'd still smell of grass clippings and gasoline from my job as a landscaper. Whirly's was always cool and dark and the jukebox played constantly: "Bad Moon Rising," "The Letter," "Hot Fun In The Summertime," "Ohio," the Crosby, Stills and Nash rock hymn about the four students who were gunned down at nearby Kent State University four months earlier, in May.

Three of my friends were at Kent on the green that day, but none were hit. One, Danny Carter, had what a doctor had referred to as a psychic break. He lay there on the grass while hundreds of bullets flew past his head for what my other two friends said was an eternity. Danny cracked because one of the students who got shot died right next to him.

One night earlier that summer, a couple of weeks after my eigh-teenth birthday, Charlie ordered two shots of Jack Daniel's and beers.

"Time for you to learn to be a man, Casey," he'd said.

From then on, when I'd meet Charlie at Whirly's, we took turns shouting out, "A couple of shots of Jack and Stroh's, Ernie." Ernie Whirly, a small, sour man with oily, ink-black hair and a cigar per-manently attached to his mouth would say, "Two boilermakers for the two hot-shots. That's two-fifty cash. No credit for nobody no offense." That was Ernie Whirly's witty expression, which he said every night to every bar patron. I don't remember anyone ever reacting to it one way or the other.

I'd felt wildly happy and free. Charlie would tell me stories of his life as a rock and roll guitarist in England the year before. I'd laugh conspiratorially until Charlie and I would roll out of Whirly's around midnight, drunk, joyous, immortal.

Now the most enchanting girl I'd ever met was telling me that a man wearing an off-white polyester shirt and bolo tie named Jack Daniels was enlightened and that I could get anything I wanted if I chanted an ancient Japanese phrase for hours at a time.

"I want you to meet Shibucho Daniels. You'll love him," she said, taking me by the hand and pulling me toward the Buddhist leader.

This was not just a touch — not like any I'd felt before, anyway. This was an envelopment of my whole life, an explanation of a question that came into full bloom at that moment: What did new love feel like? It felt like Jennifer's touch.

"How about this," I said, reaching out and touching her arm. "I'll hear all about it, but not here, not now. It's too smokey and it's a beautiful day and I want to show you something."

I looked into her bright eyes. Flecks of brown floated in the gray like fallen leaves in a clear pond. My heart pounded and the blood rushed to my groin. People chanted in the main room, Helen among them. Charlie now sat alone, glancing at his watch and drumming on the floor anxiously with his fingers. Hairball found a storage room and curled up behind boxes of Buddhist literature, candles and incense and passed out. Phil ate rice balls with the Japanese ladies who howled with laughter, the rice falling out of the corners of their mouths, as he led them in singing "Let It Be" by The Beatles. Again, the music. Again, the chanting. No chorus of angels, it seemed to me a cacophony trying only to cover the misery that would come. Chanting, music, praying, talking, laughing, eating — all of it whistling in the dark, a meaningless, bad joke.

But Jennifer Treman was real. Suddenly I believed I would go to Vietnam.

I needed to be with her outside, in the sun. I hated being in the smoky room with the dirty windows and the people who ate and laughed and talked on a glorious Saturday afternoon in September.

"Come with me, Jennifer." My voice shook a little and I was sweating on the back of my neck. "If you come with me, that would make me happy." I couldn't smile. I had never felt more serious, more desperate.

I heard Charlie call out forlornly as Jennifer and I ran down the concrete stairs and onto the sticky blacktop parking lot. I pretended that I didn't hear him. I didn't care about him. I left my bored friend standing at the top of the stairs, waiting for his wife to learn the chant that she would use to try to save her husband from going off to war.

# 3.
# River

~~~

**B**y five-thirty the air had cooled at Little Meadow. Along the south bank, on the opposite side of the river from the farmhouse, fragrant Hemlock seedlings dotted the soft black earth. Behind them and farther up the bank, white birch and Norway maples had just begun to turn yellow and red. Withering stalks of wild rhubarb wound through the woods like fences; a field of chicory, yellow foxglove, sweet cicely and wood fern covered an area the size of half a football field with five-foot-tall growth. Scattered evergreens had long ago forced their way through the canopy of deciduous leaves. The sweet, dry, bitter smell of the approaching autumn hung like incense in the air, a smell that had always excited me without reason, a smell that meant death and dormancy and cold would soon own the woods until the next spring.

The woodland areas around Chestnut Falls had comforted me for as long as I could remember, given me quiet and solace and, in some way, friendship. The woods, the rolling hills, the streams and rivers were kind and old. No forbidding mountains rose angrily above cloud and tree-line; no foaming rapids issued challenge against madly paddling athletes.

Neither were the woods filled with anything particularly nasty. The mosquitoes were benign compared to the insanity-making black flies of the White Mountains of New Hampshire; the deer and squirrels were no match for the bears of the Rocky Mountains. My woods were gentle, the smells pungent, and the sunlight nearly always found its way through the trees to the ground.

On the way to Little Meadow and my woods Jennifer and I listened to the car radio and sang along to an old Herman's Hermits song, a "golden oldie" the disc jockey had called it.

"This is kind of weird, huh?" Jennifer said. "Us singing together? We've hardly talked. But you have a nice voice."

"I play drums in a band," I said. "Sometimes I sing. Actually, you have a nice voice."

Sunlight filled the car. I wished I had cleaned up the car, taken some Windex to the dashboard and the filmy windows. A football rolled around the floor of the back seat, bumping up against an empty cardboard box of Ho-Hos.

"I liked that song you sang at the meeting. 'You Are My Sunshine.' I haven't heard that since I was a kid. I used to think it was a corny song."

"It is a corny song, I guess," Jennifer said.

I turned the car and headed down the long gravel driveway at Little Meadow. Lion met us at the top and trotted along until the tires of my green 1963 Ford Galaxy, which Phil had named "The Tank," crunched and popped to a stop.

We sat and listened to the motor trying to shut down, listened to it chug and groan as it sent clouds of blue smoke out of the exhaust pipe. The crickets in the meadow sang frantically, trying for their last shot at mating before their life cycle closed in on them. Lion jumped up and put his paws on the driver's side of the car, near the window, and barked. I rolled my window down and petted him and inspected where his toenails had scratched the door. The new scratches blended in with dozens of others. "Good boy," I said. "You're my good boy."

I'd bought the car for a hundred and fifty dollars at the beginning of the summer and pounded out the major dents with a hammer. Lion's scratch marks were an improvement as far as I could see. Anyway, I liked Lion more than my car.

The guys and Helen were still at the Buddhist meeting and probably would be for another hour or so. Rarely did I have Little Meadow to myself. It seemed larger with no one there. The house, empty and quiet of music and shouting and Jeff's chanting, took on a dignity I hadn't noticed before.

"You live here? In that big farmhouse?" Jennifer asked.

"That's my room, up there." I pointed to a second floor door with peeling white paint that opened to a small balcony with a tar paper floor and a two-foot-high wooden railing around it. "My bedroom. With my very own balcony. Like the Pope's."

"This is yours? This whole house? And you're a drummer? You must have good fortune."

"I don't know about fortune," I said. "I have three housemates. We share the rent. The three guys who came to the meeting with me. Phil, Hairball, and Jeff. You know, Jeff Robins. Jeff who chants."

"Jeff has such pure faith," Jennifer said. "*Shibucho* says he has faith like flowing water. Which is good. Some people have faith like fire — it's hot for a little, then it burns out. But Jeff's faith flows along consistently smooth and steady."

"What's your faith like?"

I didn't care what we talked about. I only knew that I was sitting alone in my car on a beautiful fall afternoon at Little Meadow with Jennifer. Jennifer who talked about faith in her bare feet and peace symbol jeans. Jennifer who smelled like jasmine. Jennifer whose lips and hair and nose and freckles made me want to live in a different way than I ever had before. Jennifer who seemed as removed from the war as anything could possibly be. The more she talked, the simpler life became to me. Light and dark. Life and death. She kept talking. We believe in individual happiness and world peace, she said. We believe in creating value and finding our own happiness, whatever that may be, she said. The air grew cooler and I thought about football games and the fresh apple cider and apples and pears and pumpkins that the crazy old man at the end of our street sold out of a wooden cart and I knew I wanted to be with Jennifer. I knew I wanted to eat Thanksgiving dinner with Jennifer, wanted to spend Christmas Eve with Jennifer. Chemistry, love, lust — whatever was happening in the Tank had taken me over and I had no desire to stop it.

Yet the possibility existed that none of those things would happen, the possibility that I would be too confused or ashamed or patriotic or scared to go to Canada or jail and that I would end up in Vietnam. The sun sank lower and the grass in the meadow grew darker.

". . . So I became a Buddhist. I mean, I've always felt like I was different, like I was dropped here from outer space. It's the first time I felt like I belonged anywhere. Life makes sense to me now, at least a little bit."

She turned and looked at me with translucent eyes like melting ice. We moved toward each other with no awkwardness. Her lips were hot and her tongue was cool as it traced the outline of my own tongue. I kissed her nose, eyes, forehead, cheek, neck, shoulder. We kept our eyes open.

"My heart's beating so fast," Jennifer said.

"Let's go to the river," I said.

We walked down the path to the river bank as fast as we could move without actually running. The leathery soles of her feet skimmed across grass, then dirt, then mud, and finally over the pine needle and moss-covered path.

We sat down by a huge maple tree that hung over the river. The moss felt softer than any carpet. Jennifer kissed my neck as I unbuttoned my shirt and unzipped my pants. "Let me," she said. She untied my worn desert boots, and one at a time took them off and threw them a few feet into some scrub oak and Christmas fern. One of them hit a decaying log and sent the damp, decomposed wood into the air, filling it with the smell of rich musk. She took off my socks, my jeans, then my faded red and blue checked shirt, a hand-me-down from my father.

"Boxer shorts. Interesting," she said, removing them quickly.

I took Jennifer's white cotton top off and touched her right breast. It was small and firm and I kissed her nipple, then moved my tongue to her stomach. "My side," she said. "My side's the most sensitive spot on my body. Kiss me there."

"Here?" I sucked lightly on her right side, just above her hip, under her bottom rib. I touched a small mole under her left breast.

Jennifer began a long cooing sound, a new sound to me, as if I was hearing an exotic new bird for the first time.

"Keep doing that," she said.

I unbuttoned her jeans and slid my hand over her pubic hair as I kissed her side. I lightly touched her there for a minute, then cupped her vagina. My mind stopped racing; something awakened.

I pulled her jeans off along with her gray cotton underpants and began touching her lightly and kept my mouth on her side. She raised her body off the moss and and shook her head back and forth, covering her face with blond hair. I thought she was crying. I had never been with a woman having an orgasm before.

Then she said, "Make love to me."

I lifted my body up and entered her. Her long, smooth torso flowed like a wave and I followed her movement. I held her head in my hands and looked at her. We kissed softly, then harder, then softly again. Our bodies were drenched with sweat as we pressed against each other. A bomb seemed to go off in my groin; I shook my head back and forth and we both cried out and then became quiet.

We rolled over and Jennifer lay on top of me and I stayed hard for a long time as we kissed and stroked each other's face and hair.

At last she took me out of her and lay down beside me. The cool air felt good against my sweat-covered body. The river flowed over the smooth rocks, east to west, a thousand sounds converging into one exquisite water symphony. Tree frogs chirped and two mourning doves made their sad, owl-like call from high up on a fir tree.

"Do Buddhists believe in heaven?" I asked her.

"Heaven and hell are on earth, depending on what you do with your life."

"I believe that," I said. My left hand stroked the cooling moss, my right Jennifer's warm hand. "Because this is heaven. I can't possibly imagine anything better than right now. If that makes me a Buddhist . . . ."

We began kissing again, long and passionate and hard. She climbed on top of me. Our bodies had dried from the breeze but her vagina had again become wet and she put me in her and we moved in a circular, side-to-side motion. My fingertips lightly touched her buttocks and back. I put my hands on her shoulders, freeing her right hand. Jennifer took her left hand and began rubbing herself in the same circular motion while her right hand rested on my shoulder, propping her up. She grabbed at my hair, put her fingers on my face, on my lips, in my mouth. Her vagina tightened around me and she held my shoulders and her entire body shook. She closed her eyes and made no sound but for long, deep, breathing.

On a cool autumn night, a quarter moon shone down on the riverbank, the river rushed toward Lake Erie, and the smell of death floated down like snowflakes from heaven. The last inlet to my childhood flooded over the riverbank and disappeared.

# 4.

# Rain

❧

**R**ain fell steadily on Sunday.

Jennifer's back muscles curved down to her buttocks in two smooth and rounded ridges. I ran my fingers down the elegant ravine that divided them and wondered if it would be a good idea to die now.

Would it be, with the rain splashing on the tar paper balcony and the moist air coming in through the window and Jennifer beginning to stir as I parted the honey-colored hair that streamed down her back, would it be, I asked myself, any better than this, ever, even if I didn't go to Vietnam? If I lived for another seventy years, married, had healthy children, found work I liked, if there were hundreds more rainy Sundays with clouds of autumn mist coming in the window and settling on my face, should I be among the very lucky and grow old with a woman I loved and know that peace awaited me in death, for peace had found me in life, would it ever be better than this moment that had been neither expected nor pursued? I had so few answers.

But maybe that was it: you found your heaven, your nirvana,

even if for a day or an hour, and you held that in your soul until your death. And that would be your benchmark, your reference, your standard for life and meaning. That was all you needed: One moment. One day. When you defined your life in the last millisecond before death, you would define it by that one perfect moment. Do we live our lives in search of that one moment, when everything works, when our body is strong and our mind is at peace and our heart merges with someone else's?

And then I got greedy; I didn't let the moment end. It melted instead into a million other moments and waited for its proper place, not in nirvana, but in the archives, among the rows of the mundane and mediocre. I took the chance that a moment like this would come again.

"A penny for your thoughts," Jennifer said.

"You're awake."

"Have been for a while. The rain's so nice."

"I'm not thinking about anything," I said. "Just listening to the rain. I listened to you breathing."

"Did I snore?"

"Your breathing sounded calm."

"I feel calm."

My voice rolled into a yawn. "I'm not calm very often."

"Why is that?"

"I've always been that way, I guess. Since I was a kid."

"And you're what now, an old man?"

The rain came down harder. Downstairs, Hairball and Jeff argued about how Jeff washed the dishes. While nearly everything in Hairball's life sprang from mess and chaos, he approached sanitation in dish washing with the fervor of a surgeon closing a wound.

"Look at this. Look at this. What is this?" Only the rain broke the long, uncomfortable pauses occurring between Hairball and Jeff. "This is dried Spaghetti-Os, is what it goddamn well is." Hairball's voice sounded muffled and low, a bear in a cave. "I'm supposed to eat out of this? It's disgusting."

Jeff's voice rose loud and high enough to come in through the air vent near the foot of my bed. "Coming from a guy who lives like a pig, that's pretty rough criticism, Hairball. I practically throw up every time I go in the bathroom because half the time you don't even flush the toilet. It's like living with an old guy with no control over his bowels. And you're worried about Spaghetti-Os? You're wacky, man. I don't need this from you." Jeff stomped out of the kitchen and out the back screen door, slamming it behind him.

"I am not gonna tell you again, Jeff. I'm demanding a house meeting," Hairball called after him.

Hairball must have been furious to invoke the dreaded house meeting —- a theoretical disciplinary gathering, a threat that no one had ever gone through with. "Wash the damn pots out from now on. Get your head out of your Buddha box and wash the freaking damn pots!" he yelled out the door.

Hairball stormed out of the kitchen, slamming the screen door behind him. His '62 Volkswagon Beetle of indeterminate color sent gravel flying as he headed up the driveway. Jennifer and I heard Jeff mutter something, walk upstairs to his room and within a minute ding-ding-ding his bell, a miniature version of the one we had seen at the Buddhist meeting, and begin to chant.

"Pure faith," I said, stroking the back of her knee, my face buried in her shoulder. "Like water."

I grew hard against her thigh. "I think I've figured out which kind of faith I am," I said.

"And that is?" Jennifer said, guiding me into her.

"Fire," I said. "Definitely fire."

I opened my eyes again. The clock read two-thirty, late to still be in bed, even by my standards. The rain had stopped and the room had become cold. It felt good being under the covers with Jennifer. I kissed her and got up to face the day, what was left of it.

I got up to take a shower. An empty green glass bottle of Prell shampoo partially floated in six inches of water in the bathtub along with clumps of long blond hair. Could Hairball be losing his hair at eighteen? I shut my eyes and plunged my hand into the murky water, loosening the hair that plugged the drain. The water made a slurping sound as the drain released. I opened my dopp kit and took out a bar of Lifebuoy soap that I had wrapped in tin foil. Every one of us had his methods for dealing with sharing a bathroom with three other guys. Having my own soap was mine.

After my shower I found Jennifer on the phone in the hallway.

"I fell asleep over at my friend's house, *Mother*," she said. "We chanted for so long that I decided to stay here because I didn't want to wake you and Benjamin."

I stood in the hallway and watched her talk. She cradled the phone between her chin and shoulder, one hand resting irritably against her hip while she played with the ends of her hair with the other. My eyes fixed on Jennifer's mouth.

"You've got to trust me, Mother. Mother, stay cool; you sound like you're on LSD, for God's sake. Tell Benjamin he's got an over-active imagination, and, anyway, I'm on the Pill, not that that's relevant here. You shouldn't act surprised; you put me on it yourself.

If Benjamin keeps shouting in the background I'm canceling my shopping trip to New York with him. Actually, Mother, Casey — his name is Casey Pedersen and he's half Norwegian, Mother, and you know how Benjamin admires the Scandinavians — Casey is a new Buddhist member. Yes, he is. I don't know, I'll ask him." She looked at me standing in the bathroom doorway. "Casey, do your parents approve of you being a Buddhist?"

"I'm not a Buddhist . . . ."

"He says they think it's out of sight — in fact, Mother, they say it's a very groovy thing. A groovy kind of love. He's feelin' groovy."

She paused and listened to her mother, then made a face and rolled her eyes. "I am not being sarcastic, Mother. His parents smoke marijuana and everything. Just kidding. They're straights like you. No, you can't talk with him, Mother. In fact, we're going to chant some more right now, and then I'll be home. Tell Benjamin I'll be home in time to watch "Bonanza" with him but that I want to go to Greenwich Village next week and not to Laura Ashley. Benjamin's got to get it through his head that I don't want to look like one of your gin-and-tonic friends from Shaker Heights when we go to Katherine's wedding. I want to do my own thing. Okay. Okay. Later is cool. We can talk later. Love you too. Bye."

Jennifer hung up the phone and walked over to me. All I had on was my bath towel, a thin beach towel with holes in it that said "Greetings from Ft. Lauderdale." She put her hand under the towel. "What's this, darling?" she said.

The way she said "darling" made her sound sophisticated, and there was all that talk with her mother about shopping and Greenwich Village, which I had only heard of as a place where folk music came from. And what did someone named Laura Ashley have to do with not going to New York City? *She knows what it's like out there,* I thought.

"You know what this is," I said, feeling my face grow hot. I didn't say that I was becoming convinced there was something medically wrong with me. I had basically had an erection since I met Jennifer twenty-four hours earlier.

"I *do* know what it is," she said. "And best of all, I know what it does."

She led me by the hand toward my bedroom. Phil emerged from his room at the end of the hall with his guitar strapped on. Little round glasses with purple lenses perched on his nose. His blue and red striped bell-bottoms rode low on his hips and he had tucked a tie-dyed long-sleeved tee shirt into them. He looked at us and smiled broadly and began strumming his guitar and singing "Jennifer Juniper," a modest hit by Donovan from a couple of years before. We stopped and turned around and listened to Phil's earnest rendition. I thought the song would never end.

"Thank you, sir," Jennifer said and clapped when Phil was through. For a second I felt bad for him that he couldn't be with Jennifer. The last thing I heard him say as we closed the door to my room was, "At least you got a place to hang your towel up, Casey," and he laughed and played his guitar again, this time a song he had written called "Little Girl Sad."

Phil played "Little Girl Sad" a lot, and we almost had a house meeting to ask him to not play it so much. All of us knew it was about a girl named Pamela Dortmunder whom he had dated briefly in his junior year at Chestnut Falls. Pamela had been pretty enough, but, more important to Phil, she was shorter than he was and had a terrific sense of humor. He lived for her, at least for the three months they dated, but despite his attentions, right before Christmas in 1968, she dumped him for a basketball player. Phil was devastated. For reasons that none of us could figure out, he wrote "Little Girl Sad" for her. No one could figure it out because Pamela seemed much happier than Phil, even when Phil was in a good mood. Jeff once commented that Phil honestly believed that Pamela was actually sad and that he was the only one who really knew her. The song was so depressing that Hairball had threatened to throw Phil's guitar in the river if he played it again, but Phil began playing it even more often, and, surprisingly, Hairball had left him alone.

That's why it was impossible to stay mad at Phil. He'd get on your nerves singing "Little Girl Sad" every day, but then you'd see him in the hallway and he'd sing "Jennifer Juniper" for your new girlfriend and smile that smile and you'd know you could never do anything but like him. And then you'd imagine Phil in Vietnam and you'd sure as hell see him dead. He'd be walking along with his head up his ass, singing one of his songs, and he'd step on a land mine or forget to duck when a sniper fired at him. He'd forget his ammunition or feel bad because he'd think about some Viet Cong guy and imagine the guy had a family and he wouldn't pull the trigger in time. Phil couldn't kill anybody and that's what you had to do in Nam. All he wanted to do was to write songs and sing them to you and walk around in his cowboy shirt and idiotic-looking striped pants and little round purple glasses. He'd cried over Jimi Hendrix and had sat up one night the year before composing a letter to John Lennon and Paul McCartney because he had been convinced that if only they would read it they'd put the Beatles back together. He wouldn't make a good soldier. You knew that. You knew he wouldn't make it for a week over there.

## 5.

# Moon

"**Y**ou have to see the moon tonight, Casey."

Hairball stood in the doorway to my bedroom. I smelled a faintly pleasant aroma of pot mixed with shampoo. Hairball inexplicably used "Gee, Your Hair Smells Terrific" shampoo, a pungent cosmetic oddity that advertisers aimed at teenage girls. His torn white tee shirt hung like a rag and he held his hands in his air guitar pose.

I looked up from my diary. "What're you playing, Hairball?" I asked.

He cocked his head like a beagle who had just heard his master's whistle in the distance, and dropped his hands.

"You have to see the moon. It's far out, man. Come outside and see the moon." Hairball's voice, even when talking about the moon, sounded menacing, so I got up from my desk and slipped into my Birkenstocks.

"By the way, what're you writing all the time?"

"Nothing, really. Bad poetry. A diary. Different things."

"What're you gonna do with your writing? You going to college or what?"

"Or what?" Hairball asked again as we walked down the squeaky wood steps and out the side porch door.

Outside, Little Meadow glowed like a pearl. A pale orange harvest moon lit up the fireweed and switchgrass, throwing off different colors than those of the daytime. Bright green became purple; yellow became gray. I felt jumpy; everything seemed to be gasping, fighting off autumn. Only the moon seemed peaceful. What grew out of the earth made me nervous tonight. What would die when winter came, what would live, what would go dormant and then return in the spring?

"Look at that moon, Casey me boy."

"It's beautiful."

We stood for a minute looking at the moon. A whip-poor-will sang its night song from the top of a white pine tree.

"They never should have gone," Hairball said. "They fucked it all up."

"Who?"

"They left a flag on the moon. The government left a freaking flag on the moon!"

Hairball turned and looked at me, his bloodshot eyes blazing.

"Do you know how much it pisses me off that the government left an American flag on the moon? It completely pisses me off, man. It makes my palms sweat."

He held up his hands. "My palms sweat when I think about it. No kidding, man, it bothers me. A flag and a golf cart and who knows what else they left up there. I mean, look at it. It's perfect the way it is . . . the way it was. Why'd they have to go up there?

All that money to put a flag on the moon? Every time I look at it now I think of it. That stupid, stiff flag. 'One small step for man, one giant leap for mankind.' God, I hate that. I love the damn moon, and they had to go and fuck it up. HOW CAN YOU FUCK UP THE MOON?"

I looked at the moon and thought about the flag that stood on its windless surface, not flapping, not limp, just artificially standing straight out. A police siren wailed in the distance.

"What about college? I thought you'd be someone who'd go to college."

I didn't feel like talking to Hairball about college. I was glad to be out of high school; the last thing I wanted to do was go to college. I didn't understand why so many of my classmates had been so excited to go off to school and study. I wanted to work my landscaping job, hang out at Little Meadow, play drums in a band, drink beer at Whirly's with Charlie on Friday nights. And now there was Jennifer, who was reason enough to stay. The idea of college gave me the creeps — all those frat boys and sorority girls. And the hippies were just as silly, full of LSD and self-importance, reading Marx while they worried about how to get some girl named Sunshine in the rack.

I decided that Little Meadow would serve as my school. Lion and I would sit for hours by the river, listening, watching, doing nothing. I didn't care about learning anything new. Everything was new, anyway: how the water made different sounds when it moved against different rocks and how the wind made a different sound when it blew through the cottonwood trees than when it blew through the ginko or oak or canoe birch trees. How the woods smelled after a rain. In the meadow and the woods I could see deer and fox and racoons and rabbits; I could watch ruby-throated hummingbirds dining on jewelweed, and black-throated green warblers and bluejays, and the red-headed woodpeckers would watch me from the top of a dead tree. If I sat near the pond for long enough I could see a waterthrush or a swamp sparrow. If I listened for long enough I might hear a ruffed grouse drumming his wings in search of his mate.

I got older every day but not much made sense. Why not sit by the river? Why not learn how long it would take the air to dry my shoes off after Lion and I walked through the river? Why not make a bed out of ferns and pine boughs and sleep while others studied?

I liked the meadow. It didn't do anything. It just grew flowers and grass. Nobody wanted it for anything. Nobody needed it for food, or to build a house on, or to fight over, or even to play on, the way they would play on a baseball diamond cut out of a field. The meadow existed, and maybe not even to be loved, like Helen thought about the sun. Pretty flowers grew and wilted and no one cut them for decoration. Grass pushed its way through the soil and no one grazed their animals on it or fertilized it. The meadow wasn't a pet or a possession. It had no needs, no agenda, no cause, other than to be a meadow.

I knew my life was simple, like the meadow. I liked it that way.

Hairball took a half of a joint out of his pocket and lit it. I watched his fingers, the flame close to his skin before he shook the match out. He put the dead, smoking match in his jeans pocket.

"I'm crashing outside tonight, Case. Gonna fall asleep looking at the moon. Gonna pretend there's no flag or golf cart or nothing up there but big old rocks and craters."

The whip-poor-will sang again, still atop the white pine which waved in the steady northwest breeze. It seemed odd, ominous, to hear the bird at night. All summer that bird — it must have been that one bird, for the song and where it came from had remained constant — had sung with abandon. Early in the summer the bird sang throughout the night. As fall came, she quieted down, finding food for her young, most likely, and in the hot months she sang only at sunset and sunrise. But she sang again tonight as if it were early summer, perhaps because of the full moon, perhaps because she would leave soon to migrate south. Later, when many springs and summers and falls and winters had come and gone, I would wonder if she had sung for Hairball.

"I suppose we could go to the moon, though, since they know how to get there," Hairball said, blowing out smoke. "We could live on the moon, set up a commune. No golf carts, though. No flags. Just my best friends. And some women. We'd need some women for sure. Think how good that'd be, Casey. We wouldn't have to deal with all this Vietnam bullshit, man.

"You'd be in charge of the music. You and Phil. Phil with his Jimi Hendrix. But you'd bring the Beatles records. What's that one I like? That album. That song off that album."

"'Sgt. Pepper's'?"

"No."

"'Revolver'?"

"Which one is that?

"The one with the drawing on the front. The black and white drawing."

"Not that one."

"'Abbey Road.'"

"That's good, but not that one. I like 'Abbey Road,' but no. The other one."

"'Rubber Soul.'"

"The one where they're looking down at the camera?"

"Yes."

"That's it. That's the one. What's that song I like?"

"Jeez, Hairball, I don't know."

"What's that song I like so much?" Hairball could be relentless, a dog after meat. I had to come up with the name of the song or I'd be out all night.

"'In My Life?'"

"No."

"Oh, man, I don't know. Let's see. 'The Word'?"

"What's that?"

"Forget it. Is it 'If I Needed Someone'? George's song?"

"No. Come, on! That song I like. The one about the guy who's all messed up."

"The guy who's all messed up?"

"Messed up."

"'Nowhere Man'?"

"Nowhere Man. Yes!" Hairball began jumping, dancing, shaking his head and singing in his two-note growl. "Nowhere man, please listen, you better listen, nowhere man, just listen, hey, listen, hey listen."

Hairball rarely got beyond the first few lines of any song if he liked it. He tended to repeat the first words over and over, ignoring any of the lines after the first. It gave him some kind of mantra-induced peace of mind, like Jeff's chanting, I guessed.

"Well, that's it," I said. "Glad to be of service. Have a nice sleep."

The moon shone so brightly and vividly that you could make out the curve of its surface, at least it looked that way. I imagined a flag and a golf cart up there. I had never thought about what the purpose of those things was until Hairball brought it up.

Hairball would never go to Nam; I was sure of that. He'd do something to get out; even if he got drafted and took his physical he'd blow the draft board's collective mind. I imagined Hairball at Little Meadow forever. He grew out of it: wild, with no apparent purpose.

I left Hairball to his manic mantric singing. I walked toward the house and stopped to rub some white pine needles on my fingers. The evergreen smelled fresh and alive. The needles were long and soft to the touch. I looked back at Hairball. The moon had risen higher and Little Meadow was even brighter. The wind picked up Hairball's singing and blew it away. By the time I got up to the house he had become a silvery ghost dancing in the moonlight, a nowhere man longing to live on the moon.

## 6.
# Wait

That autumn, Jennifer became my teacher. I was an eager beginner, she knew that, so she tuned me to her sexual frequency. She taught me how not to put all my weight on her when we were in the missionary position. How to tease her to orgasm with my tongue. How to hold my own orgasm back for longer than fifteen seconds. She taught me to pay as much attention to the insides of her elbows and knees as to her breasts.

We made love to music. She liked classical — Debussy, Rachmaninoff, Beethoven. I preferred Motown and Chicago blues and an old Sinatra album that I took from my parents when I moved out called "No One Cares," a record full of post-World War Two songs of disillusionment and heartache.

My favorite Sinatra song on the album was a strange tune called "A Cottage For Sale." Sinatra sings it as a guy who had to sell his little dream house because his girlfriend or wife busted up with him. I envisioned an earnest guy wearing a loosened tie and wrinkled suit and hammering a "For Sale" sign in his lawn because his gal ran off with some guy with more dough. He'd saved up his whole life for this run-down place and then sold it off cheap just to get rid of the memory. He seemed noble, selling his cottage because it had become too painful to live there without his sweetheart. Dylan it wasn't, but I liked it.

When Jennifer and I were inside the farmhouse going at it we'd listen to records. That was about half the time. The rest of the time we made love outside — anywhere that didn't have too many thistles or prickerbushes around and that provided a little cover.

"Slow down and enjoy the ride, baby," she'd whisper in my ear. "Jennifer's going to show you the way of the Kama Sutra."

"Jennifer?" I said one day after a three-hour classroom session by the river.

"Darling?"

"If I go to Vietnam, will you be faithful to me?"

"No."

"No?"

"No."

My erection deflated by half.

"How can you say no? You don't mean no."

"I mean no. I won't be faithful to you." Jennifer lifted herself up on her elbows, exposing hard nipples. I assumed they were in a hard condition — I'd never seen them any other way. She slid her tongue across my lips, sucked on my chin, licked her way down my neck, her swirling tongue momentarily alighting in my bellybutton.

"How can you say no? Of course you'd be faithful," I said as my breathing became uneven. "Of course you'd wait. Are you saying no so I won't go? So I'll be afraid to lose you?"

I played with her thick blond hair. My fingers fell away as she moved her head down and took my penis in her warm mouth. She knew, after the past two weeks, how to do anything she wanted to me for a desired reaction. She wanted me to have an orgasm quickly.

Afterward I said, "Maybe this isn't the right thing to say now, Jenny, but . . . ."

She looked up, her hair covering her face. "Don't call me Jenny."

"What the hell do you mean you wouldn't wait for me? Is it that you don't want me to go and you think I won't if you say that? Just tell me. What do you mean by that. By 'no.'"

"I mean no, I won't be faithful."

"It's a joke?"

"No. I mean no is no."

"Do you mean it or not?"

"Let's go to the house. I'm cold."

I sat up, put my shirt on.

"What did you mean, for God's sake? That you wouldn't wait for me. Or be faithful. What's this" — I held out my hands — "all about then?"

Jennifer stood up and faced me. We both had only our shirts on. She wore her father's old faded yellow L.L. Bean chamois shirt. I had on a cheap red and green flannel shirt I'd bought for $6.99 at the sidewalk sale in front of Paul's Men's and Boy's Store in downtown Chestnut Falls early in the summer.

I still had most of my erection. It didn't seem to be attached in any way to the pounding disappointment that had set upon me like wild dogs on a kitten.

"I wouldn't wait for you. I wouldn't be faithful. That's all I'm saying. Do you want me to lie, for goodness sake, Casey? Obviously I care about you. I'm here with you. But that's asking something of me that I can't give you.

"Come here, baby," she said, trying to hold me.

"Don't," I said.

"Don't what?"

"Just don't."

I put the rest of my clothes on and walked toward the river. I heard her say something, but the rain had swollen the river and it covered her words and I didn't look back or ask her what she had said. My insides were quivering and I tried jumping to a flat rock in the river in order to get to the other side, get away from her, and I slipped and fell and cut my arm on a sharp rock. It was a long cut, but not deep. I got up, cold and wet, but I felt invigorated from the water and somehow better.

I followed the river west, downstream. I wished Lion was with me but he wasn't around and I didn't want to go back up to the house and get him.

I kept my mind on the woods and the path next to the river. A flock of crows in a red oak tree cawed at something, probably an owl or hawk that happened by. They were nasty as hell, those crows, but I admired their unity in taking on whatever it was they didn't like.

They left me alone. I figured that they knew I was no threat to their nests or food supplies because being human I couldn't see much of what happened in the woods, couldn't move fast, couldn't fly. I must have looked like a slow, harmless creature to those sleek crows, especially compared to a hawk or an owl.

I walked fast, feeling a little numb. The cut on my arm, right above my right elbow, throbbed rhythmically. I wished it was bigger, wanted it to bleed more, wanted the blood to soak my clothes. In Vietnam the cut wouldn't even be considered an injury. For me it was almost a big deal. Over there it would be proof that I had a lucky day. I began to wonder what a bullet felt like when it hit you. Or a missile: could you even feel it? Did you have any sense of pain when it hit, or were you killed instantly? It would depend. Every death would be different; every death would be the same.

I walked fast and used a long, dry stick to whack away at the overgrown brush in my path. A couple of times I yelled out primal nonsense words and felt like I could chop a tree down with my bare hands. I used the stick like a baseball bat and began knocking over small seedlings that hadn't gotten enough sun and had died under the shade of older trees. They broke easily, letting out a satisfying crunch when my stick separated them in two.

I got too excited, though, and hit a small tree that hadn't died and the stick broke instead, half of it skittering across a patch of squirrel corn and coming to rest at the black, loamy base of a huge hemlock. I took the part that was still in my hands and threw it as far across the river as I could, shouting out the word "fuck" so loudly that I saw stars and thought I was going to pass out for a second.

The sun fell beneath the tree line and the woods changed its aspect instantly. A tiny end of a tree branch caught me on my face and cut me under my right eye. The cut couldn't have been more than an eighth of an inch long but it hurt much more than the one on my arm. The salt from my sweat got in it and stung me.

The growing darkness focused my concentration and I had to walk slowly. I knew I'd see a light from a house eventually, but I felt a little nervous.

The night was clear but moonless. I could hardly see and I didn't enjoy walking anymore. My footsteps became short and just when I thought I was in trouble, or at least might have to sleep in the woods, I heard a car going by and realized I was about a hundred feet from a road.

By the time I came out of the woods and onto the road I was two or so miles west of Little Meadow. I walked down the sidewalks on Church Street and looked in the windows of the houses as I walked. Most people had their television sets on and I wondered what they were watching. The people who still had black and white sets had an old-fashioned glow to their living rooms; those with color sets had flashing colors in their rooms that seemed less mysterious to me.

One of the houses didn't have any television set on. Upstairs, in a second-story window that was framed with lace curtains, sat a pretty teenage girl with dark hair and bangs. From her room came a light, a warm light that comes from the the inside of a house on a cold night when you're outside looking in — the warmest light in the world.

She was reading something very intently, so intently that I guessed it wasn't her school work, but instead a novel or a letter from someone she missed.

The girl in the window wore a light blue bathrobe that looked soft. She reminded me of a girl in a French movie called *Love at Twenty* that I'd seen at Case Western Reserve University in Cleveland. I liked the movie quite a bit, but I was especially crazy about Marie France Pisier, the actress who played Colette.

I also liked the girl in the window; or rather, I liked what I imagined her life to be. I imagined she slept well at night and still said her prayers and had hopes and dreams for her future.

Standing in the damp fall night, at the edge of the woods, miles from Little Meadow, I couldn't take my eyes off the girl in the blue bathrobe and I thought about her life.

I considered walking up to her door and knocking. I figured I could just tell her mom or dad that I was walking by, taking a hike as it were, and that I accidentally caught a glimpse of their daughter in the second story window, and I'd like to get their permission to ask her out. Nothing too crazy. The father would try to shut the door and the mother would intervene and say, *"Honey, the young man seems nice. Let him in."*

Their house would smell like baked chicken and woodsmoke from the fireplace. Her dad would reluctantly shake my hand and say how unusual this was. The girl's mom would ask me if I was hungry, and I'd say, *To tell you the truth I am,* and she'd get me a piece of pecan pie from her kitchen while the father invited me to sit down in the living room. A boy about ten years old would be sitting and reading in a big chair next to the fireplace and wouldn't acknowledge me. *How you doin',* I'd say. *Okay,* he'd say without looking up. He's a good kid, I'd think, just a little shy.

*Is this home-made?* I'd ask when her mom brought the pie out. *No, it's from Hough's Bakery,* she'd say, and I'd say, *That's fine with me because Hough's pecan pie is just about my favorite dessert.*

There would be a short silence and then her mom would smile in a kind way and say, *Now then, tell us why you seem to have flipped for Natalie.*

*Natalie,* I'd say. *Natalie! That's too much, because isn't Natalie a French name?*

*Is it? Is Natalie a French name, mother?* the dad would say. The mother would say, *Well, I guess it is now that you mention it . . . for gosh sakes, we don't even know your name.*

I'd tell them my name, and then talk about how I might have to go to Vietnam, and my girlfriend had just told me she wouldn't wait for me if I did go. I had needed to take a long walk to clear my head when I saw their daughter, and I'd say, *I'm struck by how much she reminds me of a young lady I saw in a movie by François Truffaut, which is why I was interested by the fact that her name is French.*

By then the father would have gotten tired, and left the room, which would be just as well because he'd obviously begun to think I was a little messed up, which in all honesty I wouldn't blame him for.

The mother and I would talk for a while. She'd tell me to call her Margaret, her first name, and then she'd tell me a secret about how she always had wanted to live in Paris, but instead, after college, she had married Bill and they ended up in Ohio because he landed a job as an executive with The Standard Oil Company. We'd be laughing and talking when suddenly the girl with the dark hair and bangs would appear at the foot of the stairs.

The girl would have put on a pair of jeans and a Texas A&M sweatshirt. *Hello,* she'd say, *what's all this about?* Her voice would have a little Texas twang to it, which would knock me out because it sounded kind of exotic.

Margaret would be flushed from the fireplace heat and the nice conversation we'd been having. *I'll leave you two alone,* she'd say. *Come on Skip, upstairs with you.* The quiet ten-year-old kid would start up the stairs, then turn around and look at Natalie and me. *Goodnight, love-birds,* he'd say sarcastically. *Don't do anything I wouldn't do, and if you do, name it after me.*

*He seems like a good kid,* I'd say when Margaret apologized for Skip's behavior, *just a little spunky is all.*

Natalie and I would talk, and I'd tell her about what had happened to me with Jennifer, except that I'd leave the sexual part out of it.

At that point, though, standing across the street, half hidden by the trees, my teeth chattering because my feet were wet and I didn't have a jacket on, I felt tired and lonely and all I could think about was making out with the girl in the blue bathrobe.

I was thinking about kissing her when the girl in the second story window got up and turned her light out and that was the last I saw of her. I waited for a minute or two, hoping she'd come outside to let the dog out or get a breath of air, but that never happened. By the time all the lights in her house went out I was certain that if I ended up going to Vietnam, and the dark-haired girl in the second story window wearing a soft blue bathrobe was my girlfriend, she would wait for me.

# 7.
# Trees

**M**y housemates sat around the white metal kitchen table. The house smelled of cigarette smoke and the liver and onions that Hairball had cooked earlier for supper. Dirty dishes sat in the sink. I remembered too late that it was my night to wash, Hairball's night to cook. To miss your turn at cooking or washing was about the worst crime you could commit against the nation-state we'd formed. We only had one house supper a week and I had forgotten to contribute to my half of it.

"Could you be a bigger jerk, Casey?" Hairball said, pointing to the sink, his mouth curled in a half-man, half-canine snarl. "Could you be a more righteous jerk? We'd all like to know."

"You can do the dishes tomorrow, Casey." Phil said evenly. "You — Hairball — relax."

"Now," Phil said, looking at me. "*What* did you do to Jennifer, son? The girl cried herself to sleep, and that was after the three of us sat up talking to her until — what time, Jeff?"

"Where is she?" I said.

"One. Until one. An hour ago. A goddamned hour ago," Hairball growled.

*"Is she upstairs or what?"*

"Twelve-thirty, one," Jeff said quietly. "We talked to her. She's nice, Casey. We all like her and we're kind of pissed at you for whatever you did, which she didn't tell us exactly, but we're sure you're at fault."

Jeff smiled. "I'm going to bed, gentlemen. Take it easy on Casey, Hairball. Glad you're home, screw-up. Jenny — we — were kind of worried about you, mostly. She said you fell in the river and cut yourself and walked off like a madman for crissakes."

"I'm a goddamned madman for crissakes," I said, thankful to Jeff for the Holden Caulfield line.

My relief only lasted five or six seconds until it turned to anger again.

*"So. Is Jennifer in my room or what?"* Bastards.

"Should we tell him?" Hairball said, smiling. He was drunk.

I wanted to smash his teeth in. "You know, screw you, Hairball," I said. "And what's that stench? It stinks like rotten meat. The house stinks like rotten meat. You cook a rat or what? God, it stinks."

"Easy, there, Daniel Boone," Phil said. "No reason to rank on Hairball's fine cooking. Liver and onions. Damn fine liver and onions you missed."

"Disgusting," I said. I was starving and wanted to eat whatever was left.

"It's just that Jenny said you cut your arm and ran off and we thought you might have bled to death or something," Phil said. "We sat up with her to help you out."

"This is nothing. The cut under my eye hurts like hell, though."

Jeff looked at my eye. "What cut," he said. "I don't see a damn thing."

Jennifer was asleep, under the covers, still wearing her dad's chamois shirt and her underpants. I took off my clothes and got in bed. I didn't want to touch her but I felt relieved she was there. I listened to Phil singing along quietly to a Traffic album. Jeff chanted his evening *Gongyo*. "*Myo ho ren ge kyo. Hoben-pon. Dai ni. Niji seson. Ju sanmai. Anjo niki. Go shari-hotsu . . . .*"

What did it mean? Did he understand those words he yelled at the box every morning, every night, day in and day out? "I'm getting in rhythm with the universe," he'd say. "Making good causes. Chanting for world peace."

Hairball's marijuana smoke drifted down the hall. I didn't like smoking pot myself. It gave me a scared feeling. Tonight I felt a kind of security smelling it. Knowing somebody was down the hall, stoned, relaxed, not caring about the things that consumed my thoughts, helped me to relax a little. I wanted Hairball to be stoned. I wished it were me. Stoned seemed like a good place to be right then. Better than where I was.

I listened to Jennifer breathing until I fell asleep and dreamed about the river.

In my dream I floated down the river, on my back, under a bright relentless sun. Lion paddled along next to me. "Lion, are you going where I'm going?" I said and laughed. The sun hurt my eyes and I worried that I might go blind. I noticed that the tops of the trees were getting closer and I could see birds and squirrels moving around very fast in the trees. The river's current moved me along faster and the tops of the trees got closer still. Suddenly I saw a flock of crows in the trees. There were hundreds of them, maybe thousands. Their heads were a few feet from my face and they shouted at me, "Where are you going?" I wanted to get to the river-bank but I couldn't turn over to swim. The river kept rising and it rose so high that the tops of the trees began to disappear. Some of the crows began to drown. They stopped asking me where I was going and tried to fly away. Some of them escaped from the rising water and some of them drowned and I realized with a deep sad-ness that I couldn't fly away with them. Lion paddled alongside of me, never changing his expression. "Lion, are you going where I'm going?" I said again as the tops of the trees completely disappeared, but this time I didn't laugh. The trees vanished under water. All I could see was the steady, burning sun. No clouds, no birds, no squirrels. I couldn't close my eyes because I kept looking for the trees and the crows, and I couldn't turn over because I needed my hands to help me float on my back. "I need to turn over, Lion," I said. "Please help me turn over. Help me turn over."

# 8.

# Bobby

"**I** haven't had a hero since Bobby Kennedy died," Phil said. He stacked the logs I'd been splitting. "He would've been president now, you know that?"

The cold air felt good against my face. All around us the golds and reds of the leaves and plants had begun turning brown as they lost their moisture. The sun traversed a low path between morning and night, as if it were working part-time. Insects had died or gone to sleep. Birds flew yet sang infrequently. Squirrels searched and dug and stocked up for the winter. The natural life at Little Meadow went on in balance, no matter how skewed we house-dwellers were.

Phil looked happy, his face rosy in the clean late-fall air. He huddled inside his washed-out blue parka. He wore a black beret on his head.

"How'd you tuck all your hair under there?" I asked.

"Ancient Yiddish secret," he said.

"Bobby Kennedy," I said.

"Yeah."

"I liked him a lot, too. Even more than President Kennedy, maybe. I never thought I'd say that."

"Me too," Phil threw a log on the pile. "I loved the guy. The man had integrity."

"You know how I found out he died?" I said.

Phil stopped stacking logs and sat on the log pile. "I've got to rest for a minute. My back hurts."

He moved down to lean against the logs.

"My damn back hurts," he said again. "I found out at school, in homeroom. How'd you find out?"

"My mom came into my bedroom real early in the morning. It was this perfect June morning, crystal clear, dew on the grass — you know? — incredibly sunny. Hurts-your-eyes sunny. I remember that.

"School was almost out for summer. I was lying in bed and when I opened my eyes my mom's face was right over me. She was pure white. She said, 'They shot Bobby.'"

Hairball had a girl up in his room and they were laughing about something. Phil and I looked up at Hairball's window. "Think Hairball's porking her?" Phil asked.

My ax sliced through a dry log.

"Do *I*?" I threw the two split logs over to Phil's growing pile of wood. "I don't. Hairball, in his bizarre way, is a gentleman. More than we are, anyway. He's probably reading her Shakespeare or something."

"Unless he ate the book," Phil said.

"Or smoked it," I said. "But I doubt that he's having coital relations with whoever's up there."

I stopped splitting logs and sat against a white pine tree. Huge cumulus clouds with dark gray bellies moved across the sun, lowering the temperature to an uncomfortable chill.

"Anyway," I said, "my mom yelled out, 'They shot Bobby!' I looked at her for a minute and couldn't say anything. She was crying. Then it hit me and I panicked and yelled out, 'Is Uncle Bobby dead? Is Uncle Bobby dead?'"

"Your Uncle Bobby?"

"I thought somebody had shot my Uncle Bobby. So my mom said, 'They shot Bobby Kennedy and he's going to die.' It was the weirdest feeling. I felt relieved for about a half a second and then angry and scared. But I got up and hugged my mom for some reason. My dad was on a business trip and my sister was away at college, so I guess I thought I was supposed to be the man of the family. All day long, at school, I wanted to hit somebody."

"He would have pulled us out of the war," Phil said. "He got killed because of that."

"Sirhan Sirhan killed him," I said. "That rat bastard didn't care about the war. But you're right. Bobby wanted out of Nam, no question."

"They're all dead, bro. Every damn one. JFK, Bobby, Martin Luther King, Malcom X. Who's left, man? Really?"

Phil looked a lot older when he didn't smile.

"Tricky Dicky," I said.

Ten minutes went by before we talked again. Then all Phil said was, "I'm freezing my ass off, man. Let's go inside."

That night, Phil went to bed early. Hairball and his new girlfriend, whom none of us had met, went to the Falls Theater to see *Love Story.* Jeff went to *Kosen Rufu Gongyo,* a meeting where the

Buddhists chanted for two straight hours for world peace.

I watched the eleven o'clock news on T.V. A water main had broken in Parma Heights. There was a fire on West 85th Street in Cleveland but everybody got out of the house in time. Cleveland Browns's quarterback Bill Nelson was listed as doubtful to start for Sunday's game against the New York Giants because of a bad knee. Two days before, the news anchorman said, fifteen United States soldiers were killed in mine and booby trap explosions in the Quangtin and Quangnam provinces in Vietnam. One of them, Gary Jancowski, was from the Cleveland area, the newsman said.

After the news, I turned off the T.V., walked out on the porch and sat in the broken white wicker chair. I thought about Gary Jancowski. He graduated two years ahead of me from Chestnut Falls High School. He played football, basketball, and was captain of the baseball team. Gary Jancowski threw a football with me up at the high school one day after school when I was a freshman. He told me I had good hands and should go out for the varsity team when I was old enough. All I ever knew about Gary Jancowski, until I heard about him on television that night, was that he was an upperclassman who took a few minutes to be nice to some kid he didn't even know.

# 9.

# Rituals

**T**he closer the draft lottery got, the less we talked about the war. Eight thousand miles away, in Southeast Asia, things were happening that were unknown or inconceivable to us. Nixon's invasion of Cambodia that past spring had been surreal. No one living at Little Meadow could imagine that many bombs. We couldn't image one bomb.

Surreal, too, were the holocaust-like horrors of the My Lai massacre and the stories we heard talked about in bars around town about babies being bayoneted and burned. Jeff said that for us events in Nam were what the Buddhists called "a state of *Ku* —not existence, but not non-existence." We knew the atrocities were true, yet we knew they couldn't be true. Napalm and Agent Orange were words that could be in our immediate future. But spoken in our world, where we talked about girls and music and how many deer visited the salt lick, those words diluted in the cold autumn air like smoke from the leaf piles that people were still allowed to burn in Chestnut Falls in 1970.

I wanted the words to go away, and with them, what was behind them. I should be in Washington, D.C., I thought, I should be working to end the war. Instead I stayed where I could hear the river at night if my bedroom window was open. I stayed where Jennifer's soft neck would give my lips some purpose other than to ramble on about something that maybe no one was listening to after all. I stayed where life meant the agonizing seduction of one season surrendering to the next. I held to Little Meadow as a child holds to his mother.

Where normality hadn't existed, we tried to create it. Rituals were broached around the kitchen table. Should we have two house suppers a week instead of one? Jeff suggested that maybe Lion needed a companion. Phil said he could get a cat, Hairball wanted a dog. Jeff talked about picking up a mutt from the pound, saving it from the carbon monoxide gas chamber made out of an old truck exhaust pipe that backed into the hole in the county kennel. The benefit of having the additional pet was debated and finally voted down. Lion would remain the sole four-legged domestic denizen of Little Meadow. No dog would be saved.

Helen began lighting candles and incense around her and Charlie's house after she got her own *Gohonzon* at one of Jeff's Buddhist meetings. Jeff and a half dozen Japanese and American Buddhist friends came over to Charlie and Helen's place and ceremonially installed the scroll in the homemade *Butsudan* that Charlie and Jeff hammered together and painted black.

Helen's *Gohonzon* was about a foot and a half long by six inches wide, with thick, black, powerful-looking Chinese characters painted down the middle, and dozens of smaller characters swirling mysteriously about the middle. The background was tan and aged-looking, like parchment, although Helen said it was made recently by a priest in Japan. It hung by a deep red satin ribbon on a nail that

Charlie had pounded into the *Butsudan*. Helen had paid five dollars for her *Gohonzon*.

"I don't actually own it. It's a lifetime lease. It belongs to the Head Temple in Japan," she said.

Helen's chanting sounded much different from Jeff's, whose robust intonations might, I imagined, have been able to reach the Head Temple. Helen's version of the mantra — *Nam-myoho-renge kyo, Nam-myoho-renge-kyo*, said again and again — was more like an urgent whisper, as if she had the ear of an angry god whose mind she desperately wanted to change, a god whose rage could be quieted only by Helen's intimate spiritual exhortations.

Helen chanted morning and night, sometimes with Jeff, sometimes with Yuki Osaki, one of the Japanese ladies who helped out the new members, and the woman I had laughed with at the first meeting. More often, she chanted alone. Charlie tried chanting for a week or so, but his legs hurt when he'd kneel and his concentration was bad and so he decided to leave the good cause-making to Helen.

Phil added more folk-rock to his repertoire of original music. "Little Girl Sad," once his theme song, became merely one selection in a yet-to-be-recorded album. It joined "The Way Of Jenny," a light-hearted tune dedicated to Jennifer, a song that Jennifer learned and sang to me every chance she got.

"I'm immortalized," she said. "You haven't even written me a poem, much less a song. Ha."

"It's hard to write a song on drums."

"Well, Phil's a little genius. That part about 'Jenny's eyes are the windows to *my* soul.' God, that is *so* cool. *My* eyes are the windows to *his* soul. You get it, right?"

"It's just a damn song," I said.

"Closer To The Fire," a song about Vietnam, was hard for me

to listen to. The chords clanged and Phil kept yelling the word "closer." It reminded me of a bad horror movie theme.

"It releases tension," Phil had explained.

"Fuck tension," Hairball had replied. "The song's a major bummer." Then Hairball went off and got smashed at Whirly's.

The song I actually liked was "Changing With The Tide," which had something to do with Jeff and Buddhism, but which none of us quite understood, even after Phil had explained it.

"Let me try this one more time," Phil said.

Phil paused and looked at Jeff, Hairball and me sitting in the living room on the night of the first snow of late fall. We had a fire going in the fireplace on the east wall and sat around it in various hand-me-down pieces of furniture. My favorite was a filthy green Laz-E-Boy from the late Eisenhower period that once served nicely as a cat's scratching post. The lever still worked well enough and I often fell asleep in the classic Laz-E-Boy leg-up position after coming home from my landscaping job or after the arduous trek downstairs from my bedroom after a night with Jennifer.

"Jeff's a Buddhist," Phil said, looking deeply into the fire. "I'm a Jew. Casey's a . . . what are you, Case?"

"Some kind of Protestant," I said, my eyes fixed on a water spot on the ceiling. A leak? This could be bad news when the snow fell. No — we were on the first floor. Hairball's room was right over the water spot. What the hell had he been doing up there?

"We used to be Lutheran until the minister yelled about going to hell one Sunday and my parents decided he was nuts. I think we're Federated now," I said.

"That's not a denomination, idiot, that's the name of your church," Hairball said. "'The Federated Church.'"

Sometimes Hairball would surprise you with how smart he

really was.

"Then I'm just plain Protestant," I said. "Who cares?"

"My point is," Phil continued.

"What about me? I'm the goddamned infidel here for chris-sakes?" Hairball said.

"This is getting off my point, but okay. What are you, Hairball?" Phil said.

"Guess."

"Hairball, please. I'm just trying to explain my song."

"Guess." Hairball looked very pleased with himself.

"You're Catholic," I offered.

Inexplicably, Hairball erupted in a phlegmy laugh that quickly segued into a cigarette-induced coughing and laughing fit.

"Oh, mama," Jeff said. He laughed. "Here he goes."

The room blew up in volcano-like laughter. Phil put his guitar down and fell to the floor and pounded at it with his fists. No sound came out of me except machine gun-like nose breathing. My stomach cramped and my bowels felt like they might let loose. They would have, most likely, had there been anything in them. As it was they merely quivered like the rest of my body.

No one could stop laughing. I don't know how long it lasted, but it seemed like an hour.

Finally a deep, sonorous voice cut through the room and the laughter.

"You guys are fucked," Charlie said. He had a huge smile on his face and stood in the porch doorway.

I looked up. A little bit of mucus had come out during my nose spasm. I wiped it with my hand. My eyes were clouded with tears. Phil sat in a corner giggling like an insane person. Jeff had gone, wheezing, to the kitchen for a glass of water.

Happy groans and moans trickled out of us.

"Oh, man, that was great."

"You're a trip-and-a-half, Hairball."

"I don't know what was funny. What were we just laughing about?"

"You guys are really fucked," Charlie said again, still smiling.

The room quieted down. Hairball coughed. He sounded horrible.

"Actually, Charlie," Phil said, suddenly very serious, "we're all fucked."

Hairball never did tell us what his religion was or what he found funny about the word "Catholic."

Charlie and I stayed up and talked with Phil, but Phil gave up on a detailed explanation for "Changing With The Tide." He gave it a quick summary instead: "It's about religion, how we're all the same, but the tides come and go and everything changes. So even though we're the same, we get caught up in different waves of religion, war, whatever . . . ."

"That sounds good," I said, but I could see the disappointment on Phil's face by my tepid reaction.

I tried to be helpful to Phil, to listen to his music and be critical, or at least enthusiastic, but my concentration had become as weak as Charlie's. That night Phil didn't sing and play his guitar before he went to sleep. He played a Joni Mitchell album instead. I lay in bed and listened to her soothing voice come down the hallway. I kept my bedroom door open, which I rarely did. I wanted to hear everything, smell everything. Joni Mitchell sang, Hairball smoked, Jeff chanted quietly until late in the night and I tried to pray but right after "Dear God" I ended up thinking about Jennifer and Helen and wondered why life was so horrible and wonderful.

# 10.

# Whirly's

꩜

**W**hen I wasn't working planting trees or doing fall clean-ups at my landscaping job I was in the woods with Lion or with Jennifer in bed. Otherwise, the draft lottery consumed my thoughts. I'd look at Phil and see him bleeding to death in a ditch in Nam, I'd see Hairball in Canada, Jeff in jail. Charlie — I couldn't see Charlie anywhere but with Helen, at Little Meadow. Theirs were the only lives that made sense to me.

Charlie and I began drinking more at Whirly's in downtown Chestnut Falls. The bar was filled with all types — bikers, Kent State college kids home for the night or the weekend, businessmen throwing a few back before going home to the wife and kids to watch "Rowan & Martin's Laugh-In," and the townies.

Despite the fact that Charlie and I lived in town we refused to think of ourselves as townies.

"Never be a townie, Casey," Charlie said more than once.

"For sure," I replied, oblivious to the irony.

Friday night drinking, once our weekly ritual, became Thursday, Friday and Saturday night drinking, sometimes more often. We stuck pretty much with beer — Pabst, Stroh's, Rolling Rock. Sometimes we drank whiskey — Jack Daniel's or, if Hairball joined us, George Dickell. "Me pappy and me grandpappy are George Dickell men," he'd say cheerfully.

Helen usually stayed home and chanted or went to Buddhist meetings. In front of her *Butsudan* she kept a piece of paper in an envelope into which Charlie had surreptitiously peeked. The list of Helen's wishes read:

1. *World Peace*
2. *Charlie to have high draft number*
3. *Health of President Ikeda*
4. *Charlie to chant*

"President Ikeda's the head of the Buddhists," Charlie said over his third Jack and Stroh's. "A chubby-cheeked Japanese guy. Looks harmless enough. Helen's got his picture up next to her *Gohonzon*."

"Is he their priest?"

"Not really. Helen says they've got priests but Ikeda's the head of the lay organization."

We tossed back a Jack and Stroh's.

"Speaking of which," Charlie continued.

"Of?"

"Lays."

"Whose?"

"Yours, laddie."

"I can't figure it out."

"Can't figure it out or can't figure her out?"

"Man, she kills me. It's like Little Casey's a soldier and Jennifer's the general. The poor bastard can't resist her orders."

Charlie sat for a long time. Too long. I hated it when he did that, when he sat staring, aloof, suddenly gone who knew where. He'd do it in the middle of a conversation, maybe one he had initiated, maybe one that had to do with him.

Sometimes Helen would say, "Charlie's gone far, far away. We'll just sit quietly and wait for him to return." She'd usually smile and give him a kiss, which would snap him out of it. Then, she'd snap anyone out of anything.

"Would you snap out of it? Damn, Charlie. I was in the middle of a sentence," I said.

He sat for a minute more. I didn't mind as much because Whirly's had a good juke box. A new singer named James Taylor was singing "Fire and Rain." I had heard about the tune from Phil, who said it was about a girl who had killed herself in a mental hospital up in New England somewhere. I was trying to figure out how a song about a suicide could sound so pretty.

"You weren't in the middle of a sentence," Charlie said after a long while. "You were talking about your pecker. 'The poor bastard can't resist her orders,' is what you said. Specifically."

He tossed back a shot.

"And what I've been doing, Casey, is thinking about what you said. Thinking about what you should do about this pouting prep school harlot who's got that very pecker in her jeans pocket. Who is this?"

"James Taylor. The Beatles discovered him."

"English? I don't remember him from when I lived there."

"Actually, I think he's American."

"He's okay, this James Taylor." He looked at me sideways. "We should form a damn band. I'll get my ax out of hock."

"Now I know you're drunk."

"Yeah. I guess. Helen would hate it if I went back out on the road."

"Like you'd leave Helen to go on the road. Like anybody would leave Helen."

Charlie stopped talking. Down the bar were Johnny Kenston and Calvin Rondo, two friends of ours from The Camp, a development across town that had been built as temporary housing for WPA workers in World War Two, and which had become an all black community.

Johnny Kenston, Calvin Rondo and I used to shoot pool at Hugo's Inn in The Camp and play basketball at the community center. During high school the rock band I played in had a singer who had moved to Minneapolis so we had recruited Johnny Kenston to be our new singer. He had a voice like silk one minute, sandpaper the next. People had said he sounded like Otis Redding. He was as handsome as Sam Cooke, too, they had said. He had it all.

Johnny didn't look right this night, though. His eyes were bloodshot and his hair was lumpy and matted. His skin had become pockmarked.

"I'm gonna talk to Johnny," I told Charlie. "He looks pretty tanked."

I walked down the bar to Johnny and Calvin.

"Hey, bros," I said.

"Johnny looked at me like I wasn't there.

"Shoot the bitch, man, shoot the bitch," he said to no one.

He pantomimed firing a rifle. He put it up to his shoulder, calmly looked down the sight, pulled an invisible trigger and yelled "BOOM, BITCH! Y'ALL ARE A DEADASS BITCH!"

I laughed. I felt sick but I laughed. Even now I don't understand why I laughed.

"Best keep away from Johnny, Casey," Calvin said. "He ain't right."

"Johnny, you still singing?" I said. I felt everything — Johnny, our old band, the past — floating out to sea.

"BOOM, BITCH! *SHOOT* YOUR ASS, BITCH!"

Johnny turned and looked at me.

"Johnny, bad shit, huh? Bad shit over there? That's cool," I said.

"Ain't cool, man. Ain't cool at *all*!"

Johnny's eyes focused on me with a hatred I had never seen in him. I couldn't hold his gaze and looked back at Calvin.

"It's not you, man," Calvin said. "Johnny got into some bad shit in the Nam. Keep talking about, 'I shot her, man.' Damn. It's not you. Don't worry about it."

But Calvin looked worried.

Johnny had turned away from me and was shooting his invisible gun at Ernie Whirly, who blinked hard and said, "Cut that crap out, Kenston."

"You want a drink, Casey?" Calvin said. "Your man Phil told me you got yourself a fine old lady now."

"Yeah, she's cool. She's great. Jennifer. Hey Ernie — gimme a Stroh's."

"On my tab, boss," Calvin said. He knew Whirly hated it when Calvin called him boss. I loved it when Calvin called Whirly boss.

Whirly nodded his chalky white face and oily black hair but he didn't offer up one of his usual stupid comments. Johnny had him nervous as a cat.

"Thanks, Calvin," I said.

I didn't want to talk about my new old lady. Johnny was freaking me out, too.

"Johnny's father wants to have him admitted to the V.A. Hospital," Calvin said. "Mr. Kenston said he's shell-shocked, making shit up, talking crazy. He said he knew some cats like that after World War Two."

"What's with that about him shooting a woman?" I said.

Calvin was a thin guy, about six-five, and he lowered his head down to mine.

"Oh, man. I don't even want to think about that. Don't even want to think about that. Shooting a damn woman."

Johnny suddenly turned to me and shoved me into the jukebox. He shoved me hard and my back slammed into the glass. The glass didn't break. The record skipped and scratched, then kept playing.

I spun around. "What're you doing, Johnny?" I yelled. I moved toward him, then stopped.

"That's stupid, man," I said. "That's bullshit, man."

Johnny spun around on his stool, turned his back on me and the bar.

"You shouldn't have done that, Johnny," I said. I wanted to be mad at him but the anger wouldn't come up.

Johnny looked straight up and lit a Kool with his Zippo lighter. He whispered something to no one and then laughed.

"What?" I said.

"It doesn't *matter*, Casey," Rondo said, grabbing my arm. "Damn it all, man, it doesn't matter what he said. You're a fool if you don't know that."

Ernie Whirly yelled at me, "Keep a lid on it, Pedersen. One warning."

"He started it," I said to Rondo. "He didn't have to do that."

Charlie got up from his stool and jogged over in an exaggerated way. He grabbed Johnny and gave him a bear hug and laughed.

"Easy, my brother," Charlie said. "Don't make me dance with your raggedy ass."

"Charlie, don't," I said. "Better leave him alone."

Charlie kept laughing. "Behave yourself, Johnny. I'm gonna buy you a drink, goddammit. Behave yourself or I'll hold you like this and people'll think we're a couple of homos."

Johnny didn't fight back, or even try to break Charlie's grip. He kind of wilted, like a crying little kid in the grip of his mother.

"We're cool," Charlie said, releasing Johnny. "Let's drink."

Charlie bought us all a round of schnapps.

"This'll do it," Charlie said.

"Hey, man," Johnny said quietly. "You know. I'm sorry, man. You know."

"You're my man, Johnny," Charlie said. "You me and Casey here are gonna form a band. I'm getting my ax out of hock."

"All right then," Johnny said. "All right."

I walked over to the jukebox and stared into it, moving the record selections back and forth but not really seeing the titles. A couple of the bikers at the back of the bar had played so many songs by The Doors and Led Zeppelin that my dime wouldn't make any difference anyway.

Twenty minutes went by and I heard Calvin say my name.

"Help us get Johnny in my car, Casey."

Four of us, Calvin, Charlie, Ernie Whirly and I, carried a passed-out Johnny Kenston out of Whirly's. Johnny sort of woke up while we were carrying him and tried to sing Otis Redding's version of "Try A Little Tenderness." His voice was out of tune and cracked with every note and he looked about twenty years older than when he'd sung in our high school band a couple of years before.

We folded Johnny into Calvin Rondo's white Buick Electra and then watched them drive south, out of town, out to The Camp where Johnny lived with his father and four younger sisters.

I sat on the curb outside Whirly's and tried to settle down. I was sweating and let the cool air dry me off. Then I walked back inside. Ernie Whirly had turned on the lights but nothing looked lit; the room was just a brighter darkness, everything covered with a greasy film. The seats of the red vinyl barstools were cracked and mud was all over the floor. Ernie Whirly was cleaning up the bar with a dirty, wet rag that smelled of mildew and Fantastik. The smell combined with the grease from old Whirly Burgers and spilled beer and blackberry brandy and whisky and cigarette smoke and I thought I was going to throw up.

Ernie Whirly stood in the brighter darkness and looked at me. His spongy arms stuck out of his white-on-white short-sleeved shirt. He wore no undershirt and I could see the black hair on his chest and his nipples, which made me more nauseous. He had three big cigars sticking out of the shirt pocket. I had no idea how old he was — forty, fifty, sixty? He was old enough to hate us, that was all I knew. His body wasn't fat, wasn't thin, just amorphous and there, moving him around the bar, serving up drinks, taking bets from the local gamblers, yelling at the punk kids, frying up Whirly Burgers and onions.

"You young guys are all crazy, Pedersen," he said as he scraped the grill behind the bar. He stopped looking at me.

"Every one of you ought to sign up and go fight for your country. I don't know what Kenston's problem is."

I wanted to kill him. I was about to say, "Fuck you, Whirly," but he must have thought about what he had said.

"What the hell," he said before I could get out the "Fuck you." "At least you pay your tabs, which is more than I can say for . . . ." He turned sideways and nodded down the bar toward Howie, one of the better known village drunks. Howie salted a hard boiled egg and sipped a shot glass of Jack Daniel's that Charlie had bought for him. Howie kept salting and eating and sipping. He didn't turn his eyes, eyes that stared at nothing from behind his swollen eyelids, toward Whirly.

"Kenston'll sleep it off," Ernie Whirly said. Then he chuckled with that big cigar in his mouth like it was just another zany night at Whirly's and one of the local youngsters had over-celebrated.

Charlie sat at the bar and threw down a shot of Jack Daniel's that Whirly had given him on the house. He seemed sober again and I figured he wanted to get back to drunk. That was the only time I ever saw Charlie Kerrigan cry.

## 11.

# Life

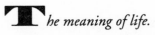

*T*he *meaning of life.*

The words awakened me for three consecutive nights. I sat up thinking only: *The meaning of life.*

How many times had I heard that phrase and dismissed it as trite? I associated it with cartoons of holy men sitting on a mountain top dispensing nonsensical wisdom to beleaguered searchers. "Oh Wise One," the searcher said in the cartoon, "what is the meaning of life?"

It seemed absurd but for the dread, the heart-pounding anxiety and fear that shot the words into my head. Lion's breathing, and one night, Jennifer's, were all that connected me to life after the words slapped me into cold consciousness.

*The meaning of life.* The words came to me evenly and silently, as pure thought, unconnected to my biology. I would awaken afraid, finally get up and walk to my writing table and write the words: *The meaning of life.* The cold wood floor on my bare feet, a floor made from trees cut sometime in the 1800s, trees that perhaps had begun to grow in the 1700s, trees like perfectly preserved Egyptian mummies, not rotted, containing an echo of the essence of what they once were, trees that now held me down and calmed me. I felt life in their death, I became less afraid, even as the night grew colder and the darkness grew longer as it moved toward winter solstice, toward resolution.

On the third night the words *The meaning of life* stabbed at me and I went to my desk and sat and looked out the window which faced west, away from the sunrise in a couple of hours. *The meaning of life*, I wrote again. Then these names:

> *Phil Rosenbaum*
> *Jeff Robins*
> *Charlie Kerrigan*
> *Jim Morton*
> *Casey Pedersen*

I sat until my eyes burned from fatigue and the misery of being awake in the cold made me groan.

*The meaning of life. The meaning of life.*

I looked at the names. I believed, there in the dark and the cold, in that awful moment, that one of us would soon learn the meaning of life. And I thought then that I knew the words to the last half of the sentence that began with *The meaning of life.* They were words that opened the door to complete unknowing, to utter darkness. The words once brought to light that revealed the darkness from which you could look back into the light, or toward the light, and know the meaning of life.

*The meaning of life*, I wrote, *is to live.*

# 12.

# Helen

꼭

As we walked by the river with Lion on a sunny day Jennifer tried to explain what she'd meant.

"What I meant was . . . ."

She stopped to examine an abandoned goldfinch nest hidden in a thicket of goldenrod that grew between a row of red pines and the river. The grayish-brown, grapefruit-sized nest was filled with soft white thistle down.

"Mama's gone. Babies are all gone, too," Jennifer said, lightly touching the nest around its ridges but leaving it where we found it. "Where are you, mama?" she cried out, looking up in the air. "Where are you, little babies? Where did you all go?"

The wind picked up soft strands of her hair and lightly brushed my face with them. She moved ahead of me, her lean shoulder blades rising and falling under her plaid wool coat. I had never seen anyone so beautiful. She stopped and looked at me, her eyes bright and secure.

*Don't say it, Jennifer. Don't say lousy things that make sense, that sound hip, that make you feel okay. Say you'll wait for me, whatever I do, wherever I go. Say you'll die for me and then I'll say that I'll die for you. It doesn't matter if it's true.*

"Casey? You with me? Darling?"

"I'm here."

I used my walking stick to whack away at a few straggler leaves still clinging to the branches of a red oak.

"What I meant was that if you go to Vietnam — and I don't think you'll go, by the way, I just don't — but if you go, I won't actually *wait* for you."

"What else is new. We've been through this, Jenny. More or less."

Her voice went up a pitch; she slowly shook her head; her hair waved back and forth, a *pas de deux* with the dried fountain grass on the riverbank that swayed in the wind.

She spoke in sing-song. "I'll just be here, in Chestnut Falls, or New York, or San Francisco, or somewhere else." Then she twirled like a ballerina, bending and lifting, holding her hands in the floating manner of a trained dancer.

*She's everything I'm not*, I thought. *She thinks she knows what's happening in her life. She'll always be fine.*

"Now listen, darling, because I love you." She let out a long breath that blew across my face, sweet as an apple.

"If we're meant to be together, we will be," she sang. "I mean, that would be beautiful, that would be cool. That would be out of sight and so wonderful! That would be our karma."

Jennifer looked at me. I closed my eyes.

"But I won't force it, do you see? I'll chant for you every day instead. And I want you to chant for yourself, so you make the right causes, no matter where you go, or what you do. And if you do that? Casey? If you do that, you'll get the right effect, and so will I. If we're supposed to be together, we will be. But for me to say 'I'll *wait* for you,' like it's from a script in some old black and white movie, darling — no way."

"I like black and white movies." I imagined my heart, black and cold.

"I know you do." She let out a little laugh. "You like black and white movies. You like Frank Sinatra, and you know what else? You like Romeo and Juliet better than Hamlet, God help you, and you're corny as *hell*, Casey, in a strange way. You like screwing to candlelight and Abbey Road *but* you don't smoke pot and you're so damned *serious* and I don't know *what* to make of you."

I kept my eyes closed. Jennifer put her black wool-mittened hands on my face. "Oh, my, Casey. Look at you. You barely shave. You look like you're twelve, sometimes. You're so confused, and you don't fit in anywhere very well, darling."

I opened my eyes and looked at Jennifer.

"I don't want to go to Vietnam."

"I know."

"And I think I fit in fine. I think I fit in fine when I want to."

"Well, you ought to think about that. About not fitting in. You fit in less than you think you do. You know? Oh, dear, you don't know, do you?"

Eight days after my walk with Jennifer it rained all morning. Charlie went to paint a living room, dining room and hallway over on Church Street for Al Zucker, the man who owned the oldest hardware store in town. Charlie had worked part-time at Zucker's

Hardware in high school sweeping up and stocking shelves, and Mr. Zucker had taken a liking to Charlie.

Charlie now referred to Mr. Zucker as Mr. Fucker, but only to me, not to Helen. What killed me was that Charlie never smiled when he said it, but said it matter-of-factly: "I'm off to put paint on wood for Mr. Fucker, Casey. It is good work, as Hemingway might say. Clean, bright, good work. Good, clean, bright work for Mr. Fucker."

Then Charlie would get into his rusted-out sky-blue Ford station wagon with the muffler that dragged on the ground and he'd drive the mile and a half to Mr. Zucker's house. "I'm off to put paint on wood for Mr. Fucker, son," Charlie would say, giving a little wave. "Have a fine day doing whatever it is you do these days."

My landscaping job had wound down. I missed the two-fifty an hour but I had a job at a the Shaguin Nursery and Christmas Tree Farm lined up. It wouldn't start until the day after Thanksgiving, so I had most of November to worry about the draft lottery and be broke and mess around Little Meadow.

I lay in bed until eleven-thirty. Lion was hungry and paced the wood floor, his toenails clicking. He sighed his dog sighs repeatedly, a primary sound in his end of the rudimentary language we shared.

"I know, I know," I said. He put his snout an inch from my face on the bed and bedewed me with canine nasal moisture. "I'm a lazy, good-for-nothing bag of horse pucky, buddy. You deserve a better master."

He looked at me, uncomprehending and hungry.

"I'm up," I said as my feet hit the floor. "Oh, man, it's cold, boy. Let's eat."

I got two Gaines Burgers out of the pantry where dog food

shared space with light bulbs, brown paper bags from the grocery store, and an album by The Carpenters with the name Bobby Haskor and a local telephone number written in big block letters across the front. Bobby Haskor had gone to our school a few years before, but no one remembered him very well and no one knew how that album got in our pantry. Neither did anyone admit listening to The Carpenters, although I thought I once heard Hairball trying to whistle the song "Close To You." The album had become a kind of sacred, untouchable house artifact with its mysterious name on the front and the forbidden pretty music inside.

I took off the crisp cellophane wrapping and inhaled the strangely appealing smell of the artificially meaty pink dog burgers. While Lion lost himself in his breakfast I ate two raspberry Pop-Tarts, perfectly toasted, a bowl of Frosted Flakes and milk, drank two glasses of Lawson's orange juice and a cup of Constant Comment tea with two teaspoons of sugar and a squirt of one of Hairball's unused Tequila lemons. I thought about leaving him a bogus note of apology about using his lemon but didn't feel like going upstairs to get a pen, so I just put it back on the butter tray next to a couple of rolls of Phil's camera film and a four-day-old, squished, unclaimed half of a salami sandwich on white bread.

Hairball had left the kitchen clean before he left for work at the chemical plant where he was the assistant maintenance man. The clean kitchen gave me a pleasantly wistful feeling of home, of childhood. I felt healthy and good. I was in my hometown, in my kitchen with my dog, with nowhere to go, nothing to do. Vietnam was two million miles away, nowhere near Little Meadow, nowhere near anything in my world.

"My man, Hairball!" I said to Lion. I held up a clean, bright green plastic bowl. "A cleaning machine is he. Let's hear it for our man, Hairball."

Lion cocked an eye toward me but kept on eating his Gaines Burgers.

I picked up the *Cleveland Plain Dealer* Phil had bought the day before. A month earlier I had stopped reading the sports pages and funnies first, as had been my habit for years. Now, I tended to dwell on the front page. In South Vietnam, the paper said, President Nguyen Van Thieu delivered a speech before a joint session of the National Assembly and said the communists of the North weren't about to settle with them and that the reds wanted to dominate South Vietnam. No coalition government with the communists. Military victory would come soon, he promised.

"We are seeing the light at the end of the tunnel," said South Vietnamese President Nguyen Van Thieu.

After breakfast I didn't want to go back to bed and I was too restless to read or write.

"Helen," I said to Lion. "Let's go find the goddess Helen."

The sun had come out and Little Meadow sparkled in the wet, cold early afternoon.

Lion and I headed across the soggy meadow. I was glad for the big rubber boots my parents had given me the past Christmas. Lion was ecstatic, leaping and racing, probably thinking our hike would lead past the east meadow and toward town.

We stopped at the Tudor house.

"Go on back," I said to Lion. "You have to be a dog now."

"Helen? I'm letting myself in, okay?"

She sat at her kitchen table drinking tea and writing on a small piece of light blue stationary. Opaque, early November sunshine fell on her. Chamomile tea mingled with the ever present patchouli oil that she wore.

"Charlie at Mr. Fuh . . . . Charlie at Mr. Zucker's place?"

"Hi, Casey. I'm just finishing a letter to my mother. Tea?"

"Only if it comes with sympathy," I said.

"You and your old movies, Casey. How's *King Kong* doing on the late show? *Citizen Kane? The Great Train Robbery?*"

"I'm into French mov . . . *films* lately. You know Truffaut? The director?"

This, I was sure, would establish me immediately as sophisticated and enigmatic, instead of just being Charlie's goofy drinking buddy. Helen would be intrigued at my knowing about a foreign movie director she'd never heard of.

"*Jules et Jim* is one of my favorite movies," she said.

"No kidding? Really?" I said, relieved she mentioned one of the few Truffaut films I'd actually seen.

"No kidding. Charlie's, too. He's crazy about that movie. We saw it twice at Hiram College on their public movie night in the art building."

"Two best friends in love with the same woman," I said. "That's a rough story. It killed me when they drove off that bridge."

"Uh-huh," Helen said. "European cinema. That must be why you and Charlie went to see *The 3-D Stewardesses.*"

I tried to stay cool.

"Charlie told . . . ?"

"I found the ticket stub in his pants pocket," she said. "The Denmark Cinema. 'Obviously rated X for enlightened adult men and women,' I believe is their motto."

Helen smiled.

"So, Denmark's in Europe, right?" she said.

I stayed quiet and watched Helen fix the tea. I felt drowsy and relaxed.

She hummed and I drifted. I imagined we were married and it was late at night. We'd drink a little tea and then go off to bed where we'd read Shakespeare sonnets to each other. No, too boring. We'd read *Lady Chatterly's Lover* or that Henry Miller book, *Tropic of Cancer* — or was it Capricorn? — and then make wild love all night long. I was experienced now; Helen would appreciate that although we wouldn't really talk about it because it would make her jealous. When I thought about making love to her, it seemed more tender than with Jennifer. Our movements would be slow, gentle, beyond sex.

Helen had her back to me as she took the teapot off the stove and poured the hot water into the white china cup. I found myself becoming aroused. She was the kindest young woman I knew, a quality that turned me on to begin with, but she was pretty and mysterious, too.

"Honey, yes?" she said, turning part way around and smiling at me. "We have no lemons."

I snapped out of our lovemaking session.

"Lemons? Hairball's got a lemon, or part of one, in our fridge, if you want me to go and get it," I said, starting to stand up, thinking better of it, starting to sit and ending up in a half standing position. Half an erection, half standing up. Caught between lust and tea and Helen and Charlie.

Helen fixed me with a whimsical look that gently let me know I had just said something ridiculous. I noticed she wore no brassiere.

She put the tea cup in front of where I half stood.

"Sit," she said. "Where are you going?"

I sat down, relieved, deflating at last.

"Here. Drink. Talk. Now that you're retired and have all this time on your hands you can amuse me with tales of your interesting life."

"Interesting, hell," I said, looking intently at the tea. "My life's mundane. You and Charlie have the cool lives."

She laughed and it sounded like musical honey. "Mundane, is it? What about you and Jennifer?"

"Bad topic."

"Okay. How about your folks? They're good? Your sister — what's her name?"

"Christy. Doing great, University of Colorado. Getting an education degree, I think. Mom's been selling some real estate since Dad's business had some trouble a while back. But they're good. I have dinner with them on most Sundays. Dad thinks the Browns are going to the Super Bowl."

I drank the tea down in three gulps. My tongue was on fire, maybe permanently damaged, I feared.

"Be careful you don't burn your tongue," Helen said. "That's that new football championship game or whatever?"

"That's the one. Used to just be the championship game when it was the NFL. Then they put the AFL into the championship game and called it the Superbowl." My tongue was raw.

"The AFL?" Helen said, looking lost. "The AFL, huh?"

She poured me another cup of tea and spooned honey into it. There was silence in the room of wondrous smells.

"Well, that's nice, you know? That your dad enjoys that. My

dad's more of a golf man. The country club and all that. In Connecticut."

"Is he one of the whale-pants people?" I said.

"Whale pants?" She smiled uncomfortably.

I heard the words come out of my mouth at the same time I knew I was insulting her.

"Those people who wear whales on their pants and go to country clubs and stuff. You know. I call them the whale-pants people."

"Is that a hippie thing?" Helen sounded sort of sad.

"No. Damn. It's just me being stupid. Sarcastic. It doesn't mean anything. I'm sorry."

She smiled. "Well. It doesn't matter."

"So," I said. "You and Charlie."

"Me and Charlie what?"

"You and Charlie are a cool couple," was all I could think of to say.

"Casey, are you okay?" Helen said, sitting down. "You look tired."

"I'm a little tired, maybe. Not that I have any reason to be. I'm not doing much these days."

"Playing any drums?" she said.

"I'm looking for a decent blues band to join. I've got an audition lined up."

"Here?"

"Downtown Cleveland. The Recliners. A bunch of older black cats. They're talking about going on tour — Toledo, Detroit, maybe Chicago. It'd be pretty cool. I'd need someone to take care of Lion, though."

Helen ran her hand through her hair, took a sip of tea. Her

face looked quiet and fresh as summer rain.

"See," she said. "That makes me feel guilty. Charlie should be playing with a band. He won't, now that we're married. He loves his music so much. I'm confused about it."

"He's the best," I said. "He's an amazing guitarist."

"God, I feel bad. You tell me, Casey. What should I do? Should I make Charlie start playing again? He's painting houses. Oh, God, he's painting houses and he should be playing rock and roll."

"Maybe. I just know Charlie's awfully happy, Helen. No one's ever seen him this happy. I don't think he really misses the music, strange as that seems. He'll play again, someday. I'm sure he will, when the time is right."

The sun rose higher and shifted its light from Helen to the back wall. She had hung a multi-colored cut glass rainbow from the ceiling. Our eyes followed the light to the rainbow. She kept looking at it. My eyes fell on her and I watched her touch her long brown hair. I wanted to know what her thoughts felt like, to be inside of her mind, to see if her thoughts were as comforting to her as just being around her was to me. My thoughts jumped around like the inhabitants of Monkey Island at the Cleveland Zoo. Her thoughts, I imagined, were as graceful and purposeful as a hawk.

"Well," she said, still looking at the rainbow. "There's something else that Charlie's thinking about. There's something else that Charlie has on his mind these days."

"Believe me, I can relate. I think about it all the time."

Helen sat straight up and her eyes grew wide.

"Charlie told you?" she said.

"Helen, everybody knows. I mean, we're all eligible for the draft. There's no more marriage exemption."

Tears appeared in Helen's eyes. "Oh, no. No, no, no, Casey, that's not it. I mean, it's it, but it's not what I'm talking about."

"What? You're not moving? Is it Charlie? What?"

Helen smiled and used her sweater to wipe her tears.

"I'm sorry," she said. "I'm emotional lately."

"Jeez, that's okay. You scared me," I said.

"Casey, do I look at all different to you?"

"You?" I didn't want to say I had noticed a few silver hairs. "No. You look great. Better than ever, really. All the guys were saying . . . ."

"Other than my premature gray hair," she said. "It runs in my family. Nothing else?"

I looked at her, embarrassed. Her breasts looked wonderful, but that was nothing new. I kept my eyes on neutral body parts — her nose, shoulder, foot.

"Nothing at all?" she said.

"I'm looking," I said, trying to focus.

Her hand had moved to her stomach. She rubbed it in a circular motion until I looked at it. I looked from her stomach to her face. Her cheeks were flushed and her face glowed.

"Well, that's good then," she said. "But you're just being a sweetheart, Casey."

I looked at her stomach, where her hand had come to rest. A tiny curve, just below her navel, rose and fell as gently as a shallow current over a smooth stone.

# 13.

# Ghost

᠅

**H**ugo's Inn was a bar out in The Camp where we shot pool. Sometimes we walked there from Little Meadow, but on a Thursday night in October Phil and Jeff and I drove there in the Tank. We were in a hurry to have fun.

We pulled in and I felt excited. Phil said, "This juke-joint's jumping." As soon as we got out of the car we heard great music, Motown music, but not just the cuts you would hear on the radio, at least not on the mostly white stations in Cleveland. Obscure album cuts, the songs the blacks listened to when they were together.

The night was electric; there was a bright half-moon and The Camp was full of the noises of its remove from staid Chestnut Falls, only a mile down the road but a cultural light-year away. This was where we wanted to be. A juke-joint in the mysterious woods.

We ordered beers from Hugo. He was part black, part American Indian, part white. He had a story for any occasion, and advice. Wise advice, ridiculous advice, cryptic advice, depending on his mood. Everybody loved Hugo. He was nothing like Ernie Whirly. Hugo had soul to spare.

Hugo was laughing and telling a story to a well-dressed chubby lady who hooted and pounded the bar with her beer glass. I watched them and felt a warm wave of pleasure come over me. Nothing could be happier than that, I thought.

We were brothers with the brothers. We were oppressed by The Man, they were oppressed by The Man. We liked the same music, hated the same war. A small, easy space to fit into on an October night in 1970. Huck Finn on the raft with Jim. Not the Jim of ignorant myth, the stupid Jim, the feckless Jim, but the Jim Who Knew. We were renegades.

We shot three games. Nobody cared who played with whom. The teams were white and black, white and white, black and black and who cares?

"You're an honorary brother, Brother Casey," one of my pool partners, Gerald Green, had said to me early in the summer. We still rode the shadow wave of our hero, of Martin Luther King, and we had not yet crashed on the beach.

We *believed* that night: That things had changed, were continuing to change.

And we kept the war away.


At about 11:15 PM Isaac Hoskins walked in the door of the Inn. Everything stopped, everyone looked up. The pool balls stopped clicking together; Hugo stopped talking to the chubby woman and the woman stopped laughing.

The blacks thought it was funny that Isaac Hoskins had a name that sounded black. "I'm English, for God's sake," Isaac Hoskins

used to say to the brothers. "Mayflower English, way-back stuff."
He would laugh with them at the absurdity.

"What's up?" Jeff said to Hoskins. Jeff told me later that he
didn't know why he said that. It didn't make sense to talk to Hoskins
right then.

Isaac Hoskins held a sawed-off shotgun. He waved it at us. He
knew Jeff because Jeff had tried to convert him to Buddhism when
Hoskins got home from Nam a year earlier. Hoskins looked at Jeff
without recognition.

"This is a gook place," Hoskins said in a raspy, distant voice.
"This is a hideout for gooks."

Isaac Hoskins was an electrician who had been in a lot of people's houses in The Camp. People there tended to think of him as
a good guy. As a brother. A brother with a name that sounded black.

Hugo stepped out from behind the bar. He smiled.

"You and I have had some good times, Isaac." Hugo said. "We
fish together, we shoot pool, we've even chased some ladies together,
haven't we?"

Hoskins turned to him and pointed his shotgun. His whole
body trembled as if it had been submerged in freezing water. He
shook hard, violently, almost spasmodically.

"I know you don't want to point that gun," Hugo said. "You
had enough of those guns, didn't you, brother Isaac?"

Nobody moved. I heard Jeff chanting under his breath and I
wanted to tell him to stop because he might scare Hoskins but
then I thought maybe the chanting would help.

Hoskins leveled his shotgun at Hugo's head. Hugo was handsome — an advertisement for the blending of races, he looked like
all his forebears and none of them. Coffee-colored skin. Hazel eyes.

Wavy black hair cut close. Long Indian nose, high cheekbones. He stopped smiling but looked like he was pouring a glass of wine. Calm Hugo.

The room was quiet. It smelled of salted peanuts and strong perfume and Hugo's El Producto cigars. Hoskins stared at Hugo and kept his shotgun leveled at his head.

"I don't know you," Hoskins said. "You're all gooks. This is a gook hideout."

"You've been drinking, Isaac?" Hugo said.

"I'm dead," Hoskins said in his raspy voice.

"No you're not," Hugo said. "You're just tired. You're a good man. A good man."

Johnny Kenston's father walked in the door, but Isaac Hoskins didn't notice. Along with Hugo, Mr. Kenston was probably the most loved man in The Camp. He stood behind Isaac Hoskins.

"I'm a good man," Hoskins repeated. "A good . . . ."

Gunshots do not sound like gunshots. They don't echo and they don't ricochet like on TV shows. They make a loud, dull sound, a quick noise between a boom and a pop. Their sound wraps around a horror of infinite depth, a sound you don't come back from, a sound that goes nowhere but into hell.

Isaac Hoskins looked like he had been accidently pushed forward while standing in line at a football game or rock concert. He moved forward a little, his head went back, his knees buckled. Momentum took over and his head snapped forward. He dropped his shotgun and fell face-first to the cement floor. I heard his nose crush when he hit.

There was a rushing sound of people, rushing to Hugo, to Isaac.

No one rushed to Johnny Kenston's father, who stood paralyzed behind Isaac. Mr. Kenston's eyes were completely clouded by tears. He held a small, smoking pistol.

"Dear Lord, dear Lord, dear Lord," Mr. Kenston said, his voice rising with each "Dear Lord."

"I couldn't let him shoot you, Hugo. I couldn't let him kill you."

He put his pistol down gently on the pool table that we had been using. His voice dropped to a whisper. "Tell me that boy ain't dead. Tell me that poor boy ain't dead."

The chubby lady who had been laughing with Hugo was a nurse. She rolled Hoskins over. We crowded around and looked at his dead face. His terrified eyes were frozen open.

Jeff, who hated guns, hated violence, nonetheless had hunted squirrels and rabbits for a few years when he was a young boy and he knew about guns. He opened up Isaac Hoskins's shotgun and looked inside the chamber.

Mr. Kenston had taken a walk to get away from his tortured son Johnny for a while. He saw familiar lights and heard the music coming from Hugo's. He'd taken his gun because Johnny's paranoia had rubbed off on him. He loved Johnny, everyone knew that. It killed him to think what the war did to his only son. Mr. Kenston carried the pistol in his coat pocket.

"Oh, man," Jeff said, staring inside the shotgun chamber. He looked up at me. His eyes were wide. He looked as if he had seen a ghost. "It's loaded."

# 14.

# Manhood

꙰

"Nothing. That's what I'm here to tell you, little brothers. Nothing. This war is about nothing, this war will lead to nothing, and unless you fools figure out what you're gonna do when your number comes up — if your number comes up — then I'm saying you'll amount to nothing.

"Don't look at me that way. That feeling sorry for me shit. I don't go that route, Jack.

"You boys gotta be creative if you want to live. Take Levine — you know Alan Levine? He's the one who wore them black lace panties and a bra to his physical and they booted him right out. I told you that, didn't I, Rosenbaum? He's one of your kind — Jewish boy. Damn straight I told you about him. Wore them bra and panties from Frederick's of Hollywood and strolled in to his physical lisping like there's no tomorrow. 'I'd love to get with all them hot boys,' he tells the sarge, 'Cause I'm as gay as Liberace.' That sergeant hustled Levine's ass out of there so fast he forgot to do the paperwork on him. Old Alan was home banging his little sweetie Marci by supper-time and he don't even have 'queer' stamped on his F.B.I. file.

"He got lucky, see? He got a paranoid sargeant, a real homo-hater. Next one coulda been one of them who say, 'I'm gonna make a man out of you, boy.' See? He got lucky.

"Man, there's all kinda shit you can do. There's this band, 'Within You Without You' — they play that psychedelic crap. They take you out for three days, load you up with speed and acid and downers and anything they can get their hands on. You go to take your physical, Uncle declares your ass near dead or crazy. Uno, dos, tres, you're home humping your own chick before The Man can look up your ass.

"Morton, don't be looking at me like that. You think you're cute with that 'Hairball' routine? It don't play in This Man's Army, you understand? They'll cut your blond locks off and you'll be lying awake at night praying a Claymore don't blow your face off before you die.

"You don't know what a Claymore is, do you? You have no idea because you're a snot-nose who thinks it won't happen to you. You laugh like that now, you end up screaming to Jesus over in the Nam. You pray that if you get hit it's either a million-dollar wound or you're dead. You pray you don't end up like me, talking to a bunch of lame-asses about what life is like with nothing below your belly-button that works. You like your dick, Morton? You think that's funny, don't you? You think having a worthless hunk of salami hanging between your legs is funny? I do. I swear I do. It's funny. I laugh all day long.

"Get me a pack of butts out of my coat pocket over there on the couch, Pedersen. Other pocket.

"God *dammit*. Thought I had a whole pack of Camels in there. Give me one of yours, Morton. You sound like a cancer ward for

God's sake, by the way. How old are you? You sound like you're ninety. I got a reason to smoke. You're a kid. Gimme a light.

"Anyway, you do what you gotta do. But forget the consciencious objector bit. Takes too long. You gotta screw with a hearing and all kinda bullshit.

"Takes too long, I said. I don't *care* what your cousin did, Robins. I'm telling you you're gonna be better off doing something crazyassed and getting out now, soon's your number come up.

"You can try the psychiatrist route. But even that, they're catching on to that.

"How do I *know*? God, you're a pain in the *ass*, Morton. I *know* because we've got a source on the draft board at the county. And they're running people through the goddamn mill if alls they got is a note from their doc. It depends. It all depends on the draft board. You want to take a chance, Morton, you be my guest. You'll be pulling leeches out of your nose before you can say Hanoi Horseshit. But you go right ahead. You give them a note from your momma's doctor friend and you see where it gets you.

"What I'm saying is you gotta be creative, see. You can't sit on your ass bitching because once you're gone, you're gone. Look at me. *Actually* look at me, Kerrigan, not at your watch. You're a big strapping kid. You wanna be like me? You don't, do you? Scares you. Then don't be a fool. Be smart, because The Man don't care about you. You're a pawn, Kerrigan. You all are. You're a pawn in The Man's game and if you don't fight back you're gonna be a dead pawn or end up a screaming rolling bastard like me, shitting in a bag. Someday you're gonna thank me.

"That's it. What, you think this was gonna be an all day seminar? This little speech is your damn reward because Rosenbaum here was nice enough to call me and let me know you fools found my record. My mamma must've left it at Little Meadow after I got shot up. She moved out of there and into this shit-hole when she found out her baby boy was coming home in a wheel chair and had to live at ground floor. That farmhouse has too many stairs in it. I miss it, though. Used to go down to the river and do some fishing. Any you fools fish down there?

"Too bad. You're missing out. Don't catch much, maybe some bluegill. Few catfish now and then, but that ain't the point. You just sit by the riverbank and look at the water and watch your pole a little bit, see if your bobber dips down and you pull one up. Don't matter if you do or not, though. It's just nice to sit there. I used to like the way the water sounded in that shallow part right before the bend in the river where it comes down from the south and turns west. Lot of flat rocks that make a *shh* sound when the water runs over it. Real nice. You know it, Pedersen? Yeah? Well, that's cool. Give it my regards. I ain't going down there no more.

"Cause I can't roll this fucker down the path, why you think, Morton? I'd get stuck in the damn mud. How'm I gonna roll this dude through the mud — tell me that. I'd get stuck and the crows would end up picking at my bones.

"Now put that record on for me, okay? I like that song, 'Close To You.' Don't listen to no loud music no more. Not since Nam. Heard enough of that over there. I was there for five months and it seemed like thirty years. Don't like no loud music no more.

"Oh yeah. That's good. That sounds nice. Don't be laughing at me, Morton. That chick's got a nice voice. Someday you'll understand. You don't need no loud music to prove your manhood. Don't tell me about proving your manhood."

# 15.

# Silence

꙳

No more. That's what I thought when we left Bobby Haskor's house, his "shit-hole" as he called it. *No more, God or Buddha, or whoever, whatever you are, or are not. Because I don't know anything, I can't figure anything out. No more, no more, no more.*

I stopped dreaming and slept soundly for the first time in months. The world shrank to a forty-acre plot of snow-covered meadow and frosted woodlands. The quiet of the woods cushioned my mind, and my anxiety about the war vanished like the songbirds. I wrote in my diary:

>A tree bends and moans. A family of deer stops and stares at me. They are silent. None of us move.
>
>There are three deer. I don't know if they're a family but I think they are. A doe mother. Her face is beautiful. She has no antlers. The buck father has large antlers, maybe a yard wide. Their fawn is spotted and small. All of them are brown, with white marks on the

*undersides of their tails and black markings on the sides of their faces.*

*Above me a gray birch tree creaks and snow falls in soft chunks. Some of the snow hits me and breaks apart. The snow is cold against my face and it starts to melt. The deer continue to watch me. This is where they must come to feed; they like the taste of birch trees. I am in their home, where they come to eat. I believe they neither hate me nor love me. Their gift to me is to let me watch them for a while. I have nothing to give them. I don't think they want anything from me.*

*Time stops. The deer have stopped time. I believe they have magic. I know they have magic because they have stopped time.*

*I concentrate and think that if I do this the deer will communicate with me. They will tell me something true. The deer will tell me secrets. I keep my eyes closed. There is nothing but silence and cold. After a while I hear the river running off to the south. I can't tell if the deer have left. The wind picks up and more trees creak as they sway. I try to imagine the deer but only see darkness.*

*Finally, I open my eyes. The deer are still there.*

*I am home now and I can't stop thinking about the deer. I look outside my window but again there is only darkness. I lie down and close my eyes. I open them and realize what the deer taught me:*

*Silence.*

# 16

# Rage

**O**ur lives, like those of millions of young men across the country, were in the hands of people in Washington, D.C. They would assist in the execution of the Selective Service Lottery — the system that determined the order in which men would be drafted. "Dignitaries" (the Selective Service's term) were to pull one capsule containing each day of the year on it out of one drum, and one capsule containing a number between one and 365 — 366 for men born in a leap year.

Two days before the lottery, Charlie, Helen, Jeff, Phil, Hairball, and I had decided to throw a party. Helen named it "The End of Innocence Ball."

"We should call it 'Party Your Ass Off Blow-Out,'" Hairball suggested.

That was the last reference to calling it anything.

"Buy something besides Stroh's," Charlie said to Hairball, and handed him a ten dollar bill.

The rest of us pitched in ten bucks — for me, a small fortune.

"Buy some Pabst. And you know what? Fetch a case of Lowenbrau in case anybody gets nervous about a low number. They can scarf the good stuff," Charlie said.

"Everybody'll want to scarf the good stuff," Jeff said.

"First come first served on the good stuff then," Charlie said.

"We should keep the good stuff for ourselves; you know, scarf it up early," Hairball said.

Phil walked downstairs. He had just woken up and had on a pair of white BVDs with a big rip in the rear, and a Kent State Football jersey he'd traded for a blues harmonica that had two broken reeds. A guy named Tony Comarato wanted it to impress his girlfriend. She loved Bob Dylan, especially liked his signature ragged harp playing.

"Comarato gets laid, I get this shirt, everyone's cool," Phil had said. He was impressed that Comarato had played football for the Kent State Golden Flashes. Number 24, defensive cornerback.

Comarato was on the green that past May fourth when the National Guard let loose. He played freshman football but after the shootings he quit the team and grew his hair halfway down his back. The blue and gold jersey had a crude peace symbol painted on the back with Day-Glo paint, right above the numerals. Phil wore it to bed about every night.

Now he walked into the kitchen and over to the refrigerator. He took out a Pepsi and drank down half of it. "*Damn* that's good shit," he said.

"I called Rondo. He and a couple of the bros are coming over," he said.

Phil had been listening to B.B. King and Muddy Waters records and had been talking with a hint of a black accent lately. "As *fine* as *wine*. The sweet nectar from the gods, my brothers."

"Huh?" Jeff said.

"Sweet what?" Hairball said.

"Kenston coming?" I asked.

"Not likely," Charlie said. "He's taking it easy since the scene at Whirly's. I saw his dad at Woolworth's. He said Johnny mostly lays around the house and yells at his little sisters. They're not sure what to do with him. Old man Kenston wants to get him into a V.A. hospital in Cleveland. Problem is there's nothing physically wrong with him. Anyway, all the beds are taken by guys with bad injuries. So he can't get him in there."

"Just as well," I said. "I heard it's not too cool. So, any women coming?"

"Women? Casey wants to know if women are coming to the party," Charlie called out. "Jennifer's coming, Helen's coming. Anybody else you looking for?"

"I don't know," I said. "I just don't like the idea of being alone with you guys with the lottery a day away. Very depressing. We need lots of girls here. Jeff, get some of your Buddhist honeys to make the groovy scene. They can do one of those — what do you call them, where you chant for hours and hours?"

"*Daimoku toso?*" Jeff said.

"Yeah, that. They can chant for us."

"And then we can bang 'em. I'll show them my one-eyed trouser mule," Hairball said, hip-thrusting forward. "Naw, I'm just kidding. I already got me a girlfriend."

"Who is this chick?" I asked. "Nobody's seen her."

"I like it like that," Hairball said. "Then nobody can mess with her head. You bringing the chanters or not, Philip?"

"They've been at it since six o'clock this morning. They've been pulling two hour shifts at the *Kaikan*. Hey Charlie, Helen did her chanting between six and eight this morning."

"I wasn't even up by the time she finished and got home," Charlie said from the living room, where he was putting on a Ten Years After album.

"Well, your wife was up," Jeff said. "Chanting to keep your skinny ass out of Vietnam."

"Yeah, your skinny white ass," Phil added.

"I'll be all right," Charlie said. "Don't worry about me. I don't plan on raising my baby from the Ho Chi Minh trail. I'll be right here, putting paint on wood and being as boring as possible."

Hairball had come back in through the side door and was sitting on the floor, feeding potato chips to Lion.

"It's amazing how ridiculous a dog eating potato chips looks," Charlie said.

"He looks cool," Hairball said. Lion stared happily at Hairball.

"Anyway Casey, you're not going if your number comes up, so what're you worried about?" Hairball said.

"Right. I guess not," I said.

I did guess not. But I still didn't know what I would do. Expatriation seemed strange. I'd only been to Canada, to Niagara Falls, once, as a kid, with my parents and sister.

Jail wasn't an option. I got claustrophobic in elevators; no way I'd make it in jail. I'd beat my head against the wall and crack it open. I admired the guys who went to jail for their convictions, like Joan Baez's husband, David whatever, the guy who went on the hunger strike that Baez was always talking about. I admired him, but I had to figure out another way.

The war looked wrong, it felt wrong, and no amount of God and country stuff could make me change my mind. If that made me a traitor, so be it. I sat down through "The Star Spangled Banner" at sporting events at school for two years as a protest against the war and had the shit kicked out of me by crew-cut upperclassmen. I'd had a little experience with scorn, but that was small potatoes compared to dodging the draft.

Then there were the guys who went to Nam, went through hell, maybe got injured or maimed, maybe went crazy. Or, in one of the worst double-deals in American history, the soldiers who came home to screamers and spitters and people who called them baby killers. That was real scorn. High school bullies who kicked my ass were almost a comic memory compared to the others.

I knew other guys who went to Vietnam even though they didn't believe in it, guys who despised everything the war stood for. They went because they didn't want to be cowards, or because they didn't like the idea of their friends being shot at while they stayed home and drove around and ate burgers and drank beer and watched "Laugh In" and sat by the river with their dog and played records and slept with their girlfriends.

I watched Charlie count out the money for the beer and I felt nervous. Then a rage came up in me. It started down in my feet, like it was coming through the floor. My heart beat so fast that the room got jumpy.

"God dammit!" I yelled.

Charlie backed up and drew in his eyebrows. "Hey," he said. "What?"

"What the hell are we doing? We're having a party while they pull our birthdays out of a fishbowl?"

"I heard they're using two drums this year to make it more fair," Jeff said. "No more fishbowl, anyway."

"We're all crazy. We should be doing something. We've done nothing and now they're going to call more of us and we're sitting here drinking beer."

"Correction, Cap'n," Hairball said. "Haven't bought the beer yet." He let out a long, satisfied belch and Lion took off.

"Easy, Case," Phil said. "Everybody's nervous. Jeff, go call Jennifer. Tell her Casey's losing it. She'd better tend to him before he gets too crazy."

I paced the room. We were being moved in on, conquered, and we were doing nothing.

"The pricks in Washington have put us in the game and we never said we wanted to play. This isn't World War Two — there's no Hitler or Tojo," I said.

"Hitler's in the White House," Phil said. "He just uses bombs instead of gas chambers."

I felt like I was being pumped with hot liquid. I wanted to destroy something. I picked up an orange and black plaid ottoman that Hairball had found on somebody's curbside in town.

"What's he doing?" Charlie said. "Casey, put that thing down."

I took the ottoman and hurled it across the room. It hit the wall that separated the kitchen and the dining room where we stood. Two of the legs broke off cleanly and one broke partially and the cushion separated from the wood frame. Phil had hung an eight-by-ten black and white photo of Jimi Hendrix on the kitchen wall and it fell off. The glass in the picture frame shattered on the kitchen floor.

No one said a word. We all just looked at the picture, the broken glass, the shattered ottoman.

"Sorry, Hairball," I said. "About the ottoman."

Then Hairball laughed. A one-note laugh, one second in duration, like a kid at a circus getting his first look at the elephant parade.

I felt stupid and thought I might start crying. I walked over to Hairball and put my arms around him. None of us were much for hugging — the touchy-feelie hippie thing had escaped Little Meadow. But I did it anyway for about two seconds. He smelled kind of weird, not like a girl smelled. Not nice. Not terrible. Just dusty and odd. I wanted to thank him and we both got embarrassed.

"What's your problem, Kemo Sabe?" Hairball said. "Jeff, get Jennifer over here *now*," Hairball said in mock horror. "Casey's taken his first LSD trip! He's freaking out." He laughed longer this time.

Everyone moved toward me. Charlie pinned my arms back and held me immobile. Phil stood in front of me and smiled.

"Now, look here. These are your orders. Tonight we party. We go crazy. We make love, not war. We say, 'fuck 'em.' We're not the Berrigan brothers. There's nothing we can do right now. You got that, maniac?"

Hairball slapped my face and pinched my nose. "Say you'll settle down and behave or we'll beat you to death with the legs of my beautiful broken ottoman."

"I'll settle down and behave." I laughed.

"Say you can't end the war right now and that you'll concentrate on the pleasures of the flesh instead," Phil said.

"I can't end the war right now and I'll concentrate on the pleasures of the flesh instead."

"Now chant to me," Hairball said. He spread his arms out in a Christ-on-the-cross pose. He grinned maniacally. "Chant to the

Great and Mighty Hairball. *Nami nami nami nami,*" Hairball droned like a chainsaw.

"Dammit, Hairball, cut that out," Jeff said "That's not how it goes. You'll get *botsu.*"

Charlie let me go. My arms hurt.

Hairball let his arms drop down from the crucifix. His smile faded and his face turned red. He suddenly looked like he was ten years old.

"So don't chant to me," he said.

# 17.

# Edge

᳥

The lava lamp warmed up as thick red gel bobbed and weaved in slow motion through the glass container. I assumed it was great fun to watch while stoned, but I was too embarrassed to ask any real stoners if that was true.

"So this is Phil's room. Very cool. These are the only real hippie digs at Little Meadow." Jennifer touched the lava lamp along its base.

"I mean, your room is a little nondescript," she said. "That's not a knock, darling. But really — pictures of the Kennedys and Martin Luther King and . . . . who's that old man with the beard?"

"Walt Whitman. The poet."

"Yeah, him" she said. "The old guy."

"I've got the Beatles up, too. The White Album pictures."

"True enough, darling."

She moved around Phil's room like she owned it.

"This room smells like pot. Your room smells like pine trees."

I kept sprigs of white pine on my desk, but debating ambient room odors wasn't on my mind.

"Pine trees? You've lost me," I lied.

Jennifer turned and fixed her gray eyes on me.

"Your room's okay. But this, baby, is kind of sexy. I know it's queer, but this lamp turns me on."

Phil bought his lava lamp sometime in 1968. It sat on his battered blond desk along with a multi-colored candle stuck in a Boone's Farm Apple Wine bottle, a book of poems by Alan Ginsberg, and allegedly, one of Jimi Hendrix's guitar picks.

The guitar pick had provided the housemates with mirthful controversy. No one really believed it had been Hendrix's pick. In a way, I did, maybe, but Jeff and Hairball had howled when Phil had presented it at one of our late night sessions around the kitchen table.

Phil claimed that he had traded an old Sears Silvertone electric guitar for it. The trade had been made with Gigundi Jack, an aptly named bruiser who roadied for Santana. Gigundi had roadied with some of the bigger bands out of Cleveland — The James Gang, The Raspberries, The Outsiders — and then hooked up with the instrumental rock band leader, Carlos Santana, when The James Gang opened for him in Detroit.

"Gigundi Jack got four of Jimi's picks backstage at Woodstock when he roadied for Carlos. Jimi gave them to him," Phil had said.

The story itself wasn't impossible, and Phil's casual first name references to the rock stars helped his credibility. Rock artifacts in the possession of kids like us weren't unheard of, either. I once sneaked backstage at a Who show at MusiCarnival in 1967 when The Who busted up all their equipment and had to take a two hour break. The show's promoters frantically searched Cleveland for new amplifiers to replace the ones they broke. I begged Keith Moon's drum roadie to give me a pair of his drumsticks, and he did. They were

"Premier Es" — the lightest, smallest drumstick made, part of Moon's secret to being the fastest rock drummer alive. At least he was fast and alive until he overdosed.

It was possible for Phil to have Hendrix's pick. The credibility problem came with Gigundi Jack. The three-hundred-pound roadie was a notorious bullshitter, a second-rate con artist famous for selling bags with more oregano than pot in them to unsuspecting young hippies. Everybody seemed to know about Gigundi's bullshit problem but Phil.

"I think it's so sexy," Jennifer said, looking at the lava lamp. "The way it moves. Slow and sensual."

"Opposite of me," I said. "Old Speedy Gonzales."

"You're sensual enough, darling. And you're slow enough, after the first time."

"Gee, thanks."

"Acutally after the second time."

"Gee, thanks again."

Jennifer smiled and the electric tingle ran down my body. All veins, muscles, blood-flows led to Jennifer.

"I want to ball you, darling," she said matter-of-factly.

I hated that word, maybe the worst word for intercourse ever used, but Casey, Jr., remained unaffected.

"Ho boy."

She cupped my genitals.

"Can he come out to play?"

Who invented jeans? I wondered. They're a prison for genitalia, a concrete barricade with a zipper for prison bars.

"Come out, come out, wherever you are," she said, her lush mouth moving close to my crotch.

"What if Phil comes home?"

"Don't deprive me," she said, pouting gloriously.

"Can't lose my edge for tonight."

I could have split logs with the damn thing. How hard could it get? It was beginning to pull the skin down from my stomach.

"Good lord, Jenny. I can't breathe. Ho boy."

"Why would you care about losing your edge when you have me?"

"It's the principle of the thing. Never have an orgasm within twelve hours of attending a party. It's Charlie's sacred Friday Night Rule."

She lifted her head. Her hair had fallen over her face. She parted it with one hand, to one side, and licked her lips.

"Charlie's? Why would he care?"

"He doesn't these days. But before Helen, Charlie was a major cocker. A god. The best. And that was his rule."

"Well, I think the rule sucks," Jennifer said, and she pushed me onto Phil's bed and loosened my pants. "You know what I mean?"

"I'd really rather you . . . oh, God, that feels great." I lifted my head up and my eyes traced the curves of her face, neck, shoulders, waist, hips, legs. "You've got an unbelievable body," I said.

"I'm just glad to share it with you," she said, taking off her black sweatshirt.

Jennifer spent a few moments down south. She licked up one side, then down the other. She put the whole thing in her mouth and began moving her head up and down. As I was about to explode, she shoved my penis back in my pants and zipped me up.

"*Damn*, girl, that hurts. You almost busted my crank. Why'd you stop?"

"That's what I think of your Friday Night Rule." She smiled and brushed her hands together.

"Now you won't lose your *edge*. I'm going home to change for your party. Benjamin picked me up the *funkiest* vest on Haight-Ashbury last week when he was in San Francisco on business. It's hand-made, darling, this fringy Indian-looking thing. I'm not wearing anything under it. I promise you'll adore it."

# 18.

# Party

At six o'clock in the evening the house was quiet. Whoever was home was sleeping, I guessed. It felt as if life was everywhere, though dormant, peaceful, uncoiled. I sat down at my desk, tried to write in my diary but nothing much came out. I wrote, *The party is tonight.*

I walked out on the little tar paper balcony off my bedroom and saw one of the white-tailed deer running out of the woods that bordered Little Meadow on the west side of the long drive-way. The doe was grayer than she had been during the summer. She ran across the driveway and into the north meadow. She stopped in the middle of the meadow, looked up, sniffed the air. I thought she might be catching a scent of Lion, whom I hadn't seen since morning.

The doe looked back toward the woods. Her fawn, larger and stronger than when I saw her last, came out and walked to her. The two of them ambled toward a stand of maples and began nib-bling at the twigs and bark.

I watched them for a few minutes. Abruptly they ran to the south meadow, to the salt lick I'd put out for them. The thought of the deer at the salt lick gave me butterflies in my stomach. I was happy knowing I lived where deer ran around doing things I knew nothing about. They let me in once, gave me what I needed then. Tonight they would stay perfect and apart.

I sat down at my desk, leaned back in my chair and watched the stars come out. I dozed off now and again, thought about women and sex and wanting to live.

The house began to awaken. The refrigerator door opened. Bottles clinked together; the door shut, rattling the metal pots and pans that sat on top. The kitchen floor tilted badly and none of the appliances were stable.

A muffled voice said, "Hey, Lion, come on in and join the party. Have some beer."

So Hairball was the one to begin the festivities. *Hairball's up, first, ready to party. That's as it should be,* I wrote.

Someone turned on the shower. Not Hairball; he was fixing something in the kitchen.

I heard Phil's voice through the water, but what he was singing didn't make sense:

*Wendy, Wendy what went wrong? We've been together for so long/ Guess I was wrong....*

*Wendy?* A Beach Boys song coming out of Phil's mouth? Phil loathed the Beach Boys. "Adolescent, adenoidal drivel," he once remarked of the California group. "They're irrelevant in 1970."

I liked the Beach Boys, but they were adolescent and Brian Wilson's high parts were kind of adenoidal. But I liked them. I wouldn't have minded living an adolescent fantasy consisting of girls and stupid cars and cool beaches forever. Life could be worse. A lot worse, I'd reminded Phil.

"You're right, I suppose, about the basic immaturity of their subject matter," I had replied to Phil. "But they're good. I don't know how to explain it. Anyway, if you haven't made out to 'The Warmth of the Sun' then you can't say you really understand the appeal of the Beach Boys."

Phil, fair-minded as always, conceded that point.

"Brian wrote 'Warmth of the Sun' when JFK got assassinated," he'd added. "That's a good tune. Point, Casey."

Otherwise, he despised their sun-drenched, party-boy music. But, *Wendy*? There had to be a good explanation for this, a real-life, party-related explanation.

Darkness came. A cold wind blew in from the northwest. I wondered where the deer had gone. Where did they sleep? Did they sleep standing up, like horses? Did they huddle together in some cozy nest of pine boughs and dried leaves? Did they sleep fitfully through the night, wander here and there, waiting for the first morning light?

*Wendy*. Phil sang it for the fourth time. He was taking a longer shower than usual.

At once my ears heard something that they had been listening to but hadn't registered. Jeff was doing evening *Gongyo*. He was tearing into his chanting tonight, his voice yelping and cajoling his *Gohonzon* to do his bidding. When he finished his sutra prayers he got to the *Daimoku* portion of the nightly ritual where he concentrated on his desires and asked his *Gohonzon* — the embodiment of the universe, he believed — to fulfill them. The mantra sounded particularly urgent as he jumped on the first syllable, barking it out as if he was arguing with some intransigent cosmic bore he couldn't quite get through to. *NAM-myoho-renge-kyo, NAM-myoho-renge-kyo, NAM-myoho-renge-kyo.* What was he chanting for? World Peace? Personal enlightenment?

Jeff finished his chanting, closed up his *Butsudan,* and walked into the hallway. Mixing with the incense he burned as a Buddhist offering was a scent that spoke of our old, shared junior high school dreams. The smell wafted down the hall, out of time, an odor yanked from the mid-sixties, when brand new Beatle bangs mixed uneasily with blue blazers and ties at dancing schools where the girls wore white gloves. I sat on the tar paper balcony and knew that smell — "English Leather." Jeff had dug out, probably from some old box that contained his baseball mitt and Daniel Boone coonskin cap, the squared-off bottle of the hearty amber cologne. As he walked — no, floated — down the hallway, Jeff said loudly, with the confidence that comes from connecting to the mystic law of his newly responsive universe: "I'M GONNA GET LAID TONIGHT!"

I walked downstairs to get a beer and saw someone sitting down on the splintered green step outside the side porch.

"Hello?" I said

"Hey, ya'll. It's just me."

It was Johnny Kenston. He looked to be fresh from a shower and *he* smelled of what I thought to be Joe Namath's "Hai Karate" cologne — the house was beginning to smell like the high school locker room after the Friday night basketball game before the dance. Johnny was wearing a cream-colored Nehru jacket with a purple tee shirt underneath, black pants, and shiny black Beatle boots. He had on silver and blue love beads that hung half way down to his belt.

"Johhny. Damn, bro, I'm glad you came," I said. "You're look-ing good, man. I got to get me one of those jackets. Where'd you get it?"

"Down on Coventry, man," Johnny said, referring to the hip street in Cleveland Heights where the hippies hung out. "My man gets them in from San Fran."

Johnny took out a Kool and lit it with a silver Zippo lighter. I'd heard about those lighters — the army gave them out. It was said that the soldiers at My Lai used them to burn down the village. I stared at the lighter a little too long and Johnny caught me looking.

"You come alone?" I said.

"You see anybody else?" he said, holding his Zippo up in the air with the cover still up and the flame burning. His eyes had a mean glow to them.

"No."

"I'm sorry, man." Johnny took a long drag. Then he smiled and the mean glow softened and he looked normal.

"*Set* your white ass down, Pedersen. I ain't gonna bite you. I was high's a kite that night at Whirly's, man. Nothing personal, you understand."

He took an incredibly long drag of the Kool, like he was suck-ing that smoke down to his feet. Johnny let the thin, light gray smoke out slowly, but not for effect. Somewhere he had learned to make smoking a butt a meaningful experience, and he looked to be enjoying it a hell of a lot.

I wanted to ask him about his old man. The poor son of a bitch killed a guy. Everybody knew he saved Hugo's life, but that didn't matter. Now not only did Mr. Kenston have his tripped-out son Johnny, he was carrying the grief of shooting a man dead.

So I let it go. Johnny Kenston should not talk about his dad on the night of the party. It was unspoken.

We both sat on the green step, looking out at the meadow.

"You cold, Johnny?"

"Not really, man. It feels good. I like the cold, myself. We can go in if you want."

"No," I said. "I'm cool."

"Naw, man," he said. "Y'all are *cold*!"

Johnny let out a sharp, easy laugh.

"You take yourself too damn seriously. Y'all need to chill, bro. Life's too damn short to be worrying about everything, man."

I ran my hand through my hair. "No, I know. You're right. I hear that. You know. My old lady tells me that and shit."

"Your mama told you that?"

"Not my mother, man. My girlfriend. You know, my old lady."

"Oh, *I* see. Your *old lady*." Johnny chuckled. "Your old lady." He was smiling, looking like he wanted to laugh like crazy. A white guy trying to talk black must have sounded hilarious to Johnny.

"Rondo be coming in a minute," Johnny said. "Invited my sister, too. Hope you don't mind."

"You know I think Carmella's a fox and a half," I said.

For years I'd wanted to ask out Carmella Kenston. She was gorgeous, with smooth dark skin and long, wavy black hair. She stood at least five-ten and walked like Twiggy, with kind of a side-to-side movement. It was said that her mother, and Johnny's, was half Chinese. Carmella's boyfriend, Carl Wood, was a brown-belt in Korean Karate and once caught me in a corner with Carmella at a party. We were only talking, but he could tell by the look on my face that I wanted to get in her pants. Carl called me up at home the next day, Saturday, and threatened to kill me with his bare hands if I talked to Carmella again. I was still in high school and my mother was standing about four feet away in the kitchen. All I had said to Carl was, "Okay, I got you, okay." I felt pretty ashamed about being such a wimp at the time, but I forgot about it until Johnny mentioned she was coming to the party.

I wondered if Carmella knew I backed off from approaching her when her boyfriend had threatened to kill me.

"How's your dad?" I asked. I don't know why I did it.

I liked Mr. Kenston. He always talked to me when I'd run into him at Woolworth's or at the Popcorn Shop, where everybody in Chestnut Falls went for ice cream, popcorn or cotton candy. Edward Kenston reminded me of my dad — a real gentleman, soft spoken and polite. He must have had to be a gentleman to deal with Johnny after he got back from Nam. It must've killed him, though, to see his kid bouncing off the walls. It would've killed my dad was what I thought when I'd see Edward Kenston walking down North Main Street. And now he had to deal with this, the shooting of a whacked-out vet who nearly shot Hugo in the face. I felt mad at Isaac Hoskins and guilty because I felt mad.

"My dad?" Johnny said. "All right. Pain in *my* ass, though. But he's all right."

Rare Earth's updated version of The Temptations's "Get Ready" blasted out of the record player.

"Who the hell put this record on?" Phil yelled down the stairs. "Who in the name of all that is holy would condone the destruction of a great Motown tune like this by this lame white-boy band? Show yourself now."

Calvin Rondo appeared at the bottom of the stairs.

"What's your problem, turkey?" He laughed. "You got a problem with my boys Rare Earth? Cats can cook, little brother."

I was walking out of my bedroom as I saw Phil move back from the top of the stairs and out of sight of Rondo. He made a choking motion and did a throes-of-death dance.

"Just tell him," I said to Phil. "Tell the brother his musical taste is in his mouth."

"You tell him," Phil said and disappeared into the bathroom. The door closed and I heard water-on-water and the muted strains of "Wendy."

"Hey Rondo," I said, walking down the steps. "Try the real thing next time." I looked to throw him a Temptations album.

But Calvin Rondo was already dancing with Carmella Kenston. She looked wonderful, with her tight red bell-bottoms that rode low on her hips, and a little white tee shirt that showed her tummy. No question, this would be a great party.

The people kept coming and the music got better. Jeff's Buddhist buddies arrived and Stevie Wonder sang "Signed, Sealed, Delivered I'm Yours." Dave Staples and six of his hippie friends walked in and fired up a joint as Edwin Starr howled out "War." Helen and Charlie cracked open their first beers as Van Morrison sang "Domino." Gilbert Blakely, a Chestnut Falls alumnus and the only homosexual any of us knew, arrived with three of his friends from the Gay Liberation contingency at Kent State as "Come And Get It" by Badfinger played.

"Hello there, dear," Gilbert announced to the room over the music. "Come and get it, indeed." He grabbed Carmella away from Calvin and they danced.

Jennifer still hadn't arrived by nine-thirty and I worried she had an accident or had run off to San Francisco or something. I had expected her by eight, eight-thirty at the latest.

Charlie didn't dance so Helen and I danced three straight songs. The third tune was "The Long and Winding Road." No big deal: Charlie was in the kitchen doing shots of Jack with Hairball and Dave Staples and Wendy Winton, Phil's new squeeze. Helen and I were pals, a little drunk, and dancing slow to the Beatles was kind of nostalgic. No big deal.

Helen smelled great. Normally I wouldn't have said anything, but I was three Rolling Rocks down.

"You smell great," I said.

"You say the sweetest things."

"Charlie doesn't tell you you smell great?"

"Not his style."

I thought she made a little noise in her throat. She was already drunk. I moved closer and so did she. I moved back, but she pressed into me.

"I really like you, Helen."

"I like you too, Casey."

"I love you guys. You and Charlie. You're my best friends. You're so beautiful, Helen. Really."

"You remember that day in my kitchen?" she said.

"I think so," I said. "That was nice."

"More than nice," she said. "You were cute."

Helen's lips were on my ear and she scratched the back of my neck for a split second.

"You had thoughts about me, didn't you, Casey? You did, I felt it. I shouldn't say this. I'm a little high."

"Hey, no problem," I said. My knees buckled but I caught myself.

"Hey, Pops, you're humping my wife," Charlie said. He had a big smile on his face as he walked toward us. The Beatles had been through for who knew how long and The Jackson Five was singing "ABC." I moved back from Helen, who kind of wobbled.

"We were talking about you," I said to Charlie.

"He's great dancer, Charlie. You should be a dancer, Charlie."

Helen grabbed Charlie by his arms and swung them back and forth.

"I can't dance to this," Charlie said. "Some little kid sings this song."

"Jackson Five," Helen said. Man, she was trashed. "*Great* band. *Love* this band."

Helen lowered her head and shook her hair, then grabbed me.

"Dance with me, Casey. Before all you boys have to go to Vietnam. You and Charlie. *And* Phil. *And* Jeffey. And *most* of all Hairball."

"Why Hairball, Helen?" I suddenly felt very sober.

"Just a feeling. Hairball gonna go. *Not* you, Casey." She grabbed at my stomach, then slid her hand down. I backed up, laughed falsely.

"Not you, sweetie. *Not* Charlie, *not* Jeffey, *not* Phil. Just Hairball gonna go."

"I thought you said we're all going," I said.

"I . . . don't . . . know. What-*ever*. Maybe *I'll* go," she said.

Hairball walked out of the kitchen arm-in-arm with Johnny Kenston. They were singing along loudly to "Spill The Wine" by Eric Burden.

"Where'm I going? Not to Vee-et Nam I hope I hope," Hairball said.

He and Johnny collapsed, laughing.

Helen disappeared up the steps with Charlie trying to hold her steady. It was eleven o'clock — early by party standards. Something was up with Helen. The lottery was the next night, and I knew Helen was nervous about it, but I'd never seen her really drunk like this.

Jeff called over to me.

"Where's Jenny?" he said. "I thought she'd be here moving and grooving."

I couldn't figure out if I should be nervous or mad about Jennifer not showing up.

"I don't know," I said. "I'm going to give her a call."

Charlie came back downstairs.

"How'd Helen get so hammered on three beers?" I said.

"She's nervous, man, really nervous about the whole lottery deal. She keeps having dreams that I go, then that Hairball goes. It's a drag. I'll be glad when the lottery's over."

"Me too," I said. The hair on the back of my neck got wet with sweat.

"We're watching it together, right, Charlie? For moral support and all that?"

"Sure. Let's not worry about it now. You gonna take a shot at Carmella Kenston or not?"

Carmella was grooving to Hendrix's "Stone Free" with Jeff, who looked like he was under the Bodhi tree verging on enlightenment. Carmella was one incredible looking woman. About ten minutes later Jeff and Carmella left the living room dance floor and walked past me, moving toward the stairs.

"She wants to see my *Gohonzon*," he said and grinned at me insanely. He had his hand on Carmella's ass.

I've never been able to see auras, but if I could have that night, I'm pretty sure that Jeff's was as bright as the Northern Lights as he walked up the stairs with the regal Carmella Kenston.

I wandered. Even at our own house party, I liked wandering as if I was somewhere new. With all the booze and dope being ingested, most everybody was new in one way or another, and personalities emerged throughout the house. We danced around our fears, we raged against the coming draft lottery with the dark joy of condemned youth.

The kitchen was filled with smoke, some from joints, most smoke coming off the ends of Kools and Winstons and Newports. Dave Staples and Hairball debated whether Joe Walsh, the guitarist from The James Gang, was as good as Pete Townsend of The Who. Hairball said Walsh was "excellent, nearly as good as Hendrix, not to mention Townsend." Staples laughed at Hairball and said Walsh was a flash-in-the-pan.

"My sister's best friend dates him. My sister says he a light-weight, a dufus, he'll be pumping gas in a year," Staples said.

Rondo and Blakely sat in the hallway near the back kitchen door and talked about repression.

"The gay man is America's new nigger," Gilbert said. He glanced quickly at Rondo at his use of the word "nigger." Rondo didn't flinch, kept his head down and nodded slowly. Blakely had passed the hip test.

"I hear you," Rondo said. "But Yoko Ono says 'woman is the nigger of the world.' What about that?"

They didn't notice me standing there. Their conversation went on in solidarity as Rondo and Blakely mutually debated who could bear the temporarily honorific title of "nigger." Finally, I could bear it no longer. A little buzzed, I bent down.

"Look here. I have something to say to this impressive gathering of Afro-Americans and homosexuals."

Blakely, his curly hair hanging in his face, made an exaggerated Bette Davis motion with his cigarette and blew the smoke in my face.

"Well, hello there, dear boy. And what could a fresh-faced white-boy breeder like you possibly have to add to this conversation? This is for repressed classes only."

I squinted at Blakely and Rondo. Calvin had a big smile on his face. He wanted outrage.

"There's only one true nigger in the whole world. And that . . . is me. I'm the nigger of the universe."

I stood up dramatically and took a chug of Rolling Rock. I chugged too fast and foam rose in the bottle and beer soaked my face. Rondo and Blakely went wild. "Oh, *man*," Rondo yelled. "Casey's a *foaming* nigger!" Rondo kicked his feet against the wall and laughed. "Nigger be *foaming at the mouth!*"

Blakely shouted at me, "No *fair*, you horrible man. You ruined our discussion." But he laughed and then he and Rondo got into a slap fight. Rondo could have beat the hell out of him but he was amused at Gilbert and egged him on.

"Come on, nigger," Rondo said, laughing as Gilbert tried to smack him. "Let me see what you got."

The living room was going at full tilt. Everybody was dancing. Two or three couples were making out. I was getting pretty randy myself. Where was Jennifer? Now it was too late to call her.

Phil sat in front of the fireplace talking to Wendy Winton.

"Music is the only true language," he was saying. He spotted me. "Wendy, meet my house mate, Casey Pedersen. Casey, this is Wendy."

Wendy smiled broadly. Her brown hair spiraled down past her shoulders, ringlets hung past eyes that had laugh lines splaying out from them. Short and pretty, wearing no makeup, she was Phil's dream lover, I could see.

"Hey," she said. "Heard you're pretty hip. A drummer? That's cool. Drums are the purest form of communication. Philip and I were just talking about how language is bogus, that music is the only way, man."

"Close your eyes and listen, man," Phil said. Curtis Mayfield sang, "If There's A Hell Below We're All Going To Go."

Wendy blissfully closed her eyes and inched closer to the fireplace. Their legs touched. His eyes still closed, Phil's hand moved on top of Wendy's, who said, "Yes. Nice."

"Tripping the light fantastic?" I said to Phil.

Phil opened his eyes — they were all pupils — and reached into the left front pocket of his green-and-orange striped bell-bottoms. He took out a blue kerchief, unwrapped it and removed a tiny piece of brown paper.

"Picture yourself in a boat on a river, my man," he said. "With tangerine trees and marmalade skies." He held out the L.S.D.

"No, man, not me. But thanks," I said. "One hit of that stuff and I'm on the Terminal Tower playing Superman. Drugs and I don't mix too well."

He had his eyes closed again. "Someone is calling. You, Casey, answer quite clearly. The girl with kaleidoscope eyes — you know what I mean?" he said. "You sure, man? You don't know what you're missing."

"You ought to think about it, drummer boy," Wendy said, smiling. "It's real nice in here." Her eyes were still closed and she was practically on Phil's lap.

"Send me a postcard," I said. I walked to the other side of the room and looked back at Phil and Wendy. Their tongues were taking a trip down each other's throats.

The party died slowly. Hairball passed out on his way to the bathroom. He looked as if he had been felled by an ax, chopped dead in his tracks. He lay on his side, his right hand raised above his head, his left down at his side, like a chalk drawing at the scene of the crime. By three-thirty his breathing was heavy but steady but for his usual raspiness. His mass of blond hair lay like a tumbleweed on the floor, occasionally moving when someone walked out the side porch door and the wind blew through.

Passed out, too, was Johnny Kenston, who lay on his back in front of the fireplace where Phil had sat before he and Wendy retired to his room. Great moans and wails from Phil's room were heard for no more than five minutes, then silence. One could only imagine the intensity of either the orgasms or the bad trips. I hoped, for Phil's sake, the sounds were orgasmic.

In the post-party drift, as smoke and alcohol fumes and left-over libido wafted through the rooms, Charlie, Rondo and I sat and talked until just before dawn.

The meadow was ink black and soundless. Hairball snored

loudly in the hallway. Johnny Kenston breathed hard and babbled in his sleep. Humor had utterly left us; Hairball's and Johnny's noises could have been sources of hilarity but weren't.

Vietnam descended in our kitchen like poisonous fumes. We breathed in and entered our time again. The nausea of the unknown settled in my stomach.

Rondo talked about his best friend Johnny Kenston. Yes, Calvin said, Johnny was at My Lai. Now he wanted to die, but his father and sisters never let up, telling him they loved him, pleading with him to get help, promising him life would get better.

Johnny could not be consoled, Calvin said. He had, from what Mr. Kenston gathered, shot at least one woman in the massacre, and maybe a child. Johnny frequently cried for hours at a time. No one knew what to do except wait for him to fall asleep, exhausted by his despair.

# 19.

# Trust

꿈

**H**elen didn't move. Charlie and I talked about carrying her across the meadow and putting her to bed, but we decided we might drop her down the stairs and accidentally kill her.

"That's probably a bad idea," Charlie said.

"She can't stay in my bed," I said. "That's a really bad idea."

"Why?"

"It just is."

"Can't you sleep downstairs?"

"Johnny's not on the couch?"

"He's sleeping in front of the fireplace."

"Or I could sleep in Hairball's bed. Then again he might wake up and come to bed and that's too hideous a thought to deal with."

"Hairball's not going to wake up," Charlie said. "He'll sleep until tomorrow night."

"There's our answer," I said.

"There's our answer," Charlie said.

"Case."

"Yeah."

"I trust you. Stop acting so nervous. I don't think you're going to rape my wife in her sleep."

"I could sleep on your couch," I said.

"We don't have a couch. Two chairs. No couch. One bed. Which I sleep in. Alone, or with my wife. Not with you, old buddy.

"This was good tonight," Charlie said, turning and walking toward the stairs. He looked happy.

"The lottery's tonight," I said.

Charlie stopped half way down the stairs and turned to look at me. He stopped smiling.

I watched Charlie walk across the snow-covered meadow. He looked up at the stars as he walked. Lion followed him most of the way, then came home full of snow and ice. When he came in I hugged him.

"I wish I was you," I said. His black tail with the white tip wagged, throwing off ice.

The house was cold now and seemed lonesome in the party's aftermath. I wondered if the future would end for any of us soon. I wondered where I'd be in six months; where any of us would be. I wondered where to sleep because Hairball was gone from the couch. That could only mean he was back in his room. There were no blankets on the couch, or anywhere else, and the drafts came in through the old windows and doorways.

I headed up the stairs for my bedroom, where Helen lay passed out in my bed.

"Casey? Is that you?"

"Helen. You're awake."

"What time is it?"

"After five. It'll be getting light soon. You should go back to sleep."

"How long was I out?"

"Since about midnight. How'd you get so smashed? You only had a couple of beers."

"I didn't eat all day. And I had a couple of tokes of Dave Staples's joint."

"You?"

"I know. I don't do that. But I did. I've been worried about everything."

"I hear."

"Where are you?"

"Lying on the floor. Over by my closet, on a bed of laundry. I was going to sleep in Hairball's room, but he woke up and went to bed."

"Oh. Where's Jennifer?"

"Never showed."

"Oh."

"I was going to sleep on the couch downstairs but it's freezing. You know how cold it gets down there at night."

"Uh huh."

"Well, go back to sleep. I'm going to try to get some sleep myself."

"Charlie knows I'm here; of course he does, right?"

"He helped me put you to bed."

"Is he mad?"

"He's cool. He had a great time," I said. "Goodnight."

I could tell by Helen's breathing that she wasn't sleeping. I was wide awake. A few minutes passed and she rolled over.

"Casey."

"I can't sleep either," I said.

"This is silly. You can sleep in the bed. You're like my little brother, for God's sake."

"I am kind of cold. There's a draft under the door to the balcony." She laughed quietly. "Your tiny balcony. You like having a balcony, huh?"

I got in bed. Helen was under the sheets and a couple of blankets. I crawled in between the blankets and sheets. I still had on my jeans and a sweatshirt. If she was wearing underpants and clothes there were as many as seven layers of cloth to keep us apart.

I lay on my right side, facing away from her.

"Could you play some of that music?"

"Which music?"

"That pretty music you play sometimes."

"That classical record I have? That Bach guitar record?"

"No, the pretty singing. You know."

"The Frank Sinatra album?"

"That's it. With all those sad songs on it. I feel sad. Put it on. Please?"

I got back up and lit a candle next to my bed and found the record. There was old Frank, sitting by the bar, a glass of whiskey in front of him, his tie loose, a cigarette burning, lots of happy people behind him, ignoring him.

"'When No One Cares'. I think this is what you want."

"Put it on, okay?"

Over fifteen or so years of scratches — Mom and Dad had played it plenty, after all — Frank sang.

I lay back down between the sheets and blankets, away from Helen.

"Life's hard," she said.

"I guess so."

"I don't know what's going to happen. I have bad feelings."

"Everything's going to be fine."

"This is pretty music."

"I like it."

"I like it, too. It's cold in here."

I turned over as Helen was moving to put her head on my shoulder. Our faces brushed up against each other's and we kissed. It lasted a few seconds. I knew if I spoke, if I questioned it, if I injected any reason into it, what was happening might stop. I kissed her again.

Even with Jennifer, my first and only lover, I hadn't experienced anything like this. It wasn't happening in a slow and sensuous way, like with Jennifer.

We ripped off the blankets, the sheets, our clothes. We kissed so hard my lips hurt and then we kissed harder. It felt scary, then unbelievably exciting, as if I'd jumped out of an airplane without thought of whether I had a parachute on. I kissed down her neck and kept going. Control left me; I felt it leave Helen, too, a lifting out, an escape. I kept moving down and kissed her on her thighs and inhaled. Her scent rushed to my brain.

So it wouldn't be her mind I would enter at all, the way I had fantasized that day in her kitchen. It would be her body. I put my mouth on her vagina, licked it, kissed it, grabbed her ass with my hands and stroked hard. Her leg muscles clenched and strained against me. I wanted my tongue as far in her as it would go; I wanted my head inside her. I loved her, wanted her, would die or kill for her. This was my woman, and I would have her. I would save her because I wanted her, because I knew she needed me. A dozen reasons for what I was doing rushed into my mind, none of them articulate, none real. But at that moment I would have killed to defend my reasons, whatever they were. I would have sold out anything, anyone.

All doubts left me but one.

"What about you being pregnant?" I said.

"Don't," she said. "Shh."

"Oh, God," I said. No doubts now.

I kissed my way back up her legs and torso and looked at her lean body, at her long brown hair, at her face.

"Do it," she said.

A few second's hesitation, and then, again, "Do it."

We kissed again and our tongues never stopped. We kept them moving in each other's mouths so we couldn't talk anymore.

Something like an angry sob released from my chest. She grabbed my back and pounded on it.

As our friction became the essence of primordial ecstasy, I kept thinking: *This is the best and worst thing I've ever done.* My lust for Helen equaled contempt for my best friend's trust, and for the small, decent constructs I had tenuously put together over eighteen years. None of it mattered. I was inside her.

By dawn we had murdered the villagers and burned their huts to ash.

# 20.

# Charlie

~❧~

"**S**o, did you jump my wife last night? Just kidding, bro. Jeez, you sound awful. Hey, don't tell Helen I made that crack about you and her . . . you know. Seriously, you get any sleep at all? That was nice of you to let Helen crash in your bed.

"No kidding? You slept on your dirty clothes? I'm still in bed myself. It's like noon, isn't it? Yeah, it is.

"Great party. What's going on with Jeff? Carmella Kenston, huh? That's great. She's cool. Old Jeff. And Phil was getting down with that Wendy chick. She's cool, too. I had a good talk with her before she and Phil got down and funky. She's from Hawaii, did you know that? Father's a dee jay or something. A record guy or something, I don't know. I can't remember. She'd be good for Phil. Get his mind off his Little Girl Sad chick.

"No, don't wake her up. Let her sleep. She's preggers, anyway. Hey, Case, if you get a chance sometime, talk to her, will you?

"I don't know what about. About everything, anything. I think Helen's got a bunch of stuff going on that she doesn't talk with anybody about. She can't really talk with her mom. They argue too much. They're a lot alike. You know how that is.

"Thanks. I appreciate it. You're a good friend to her.

"I know; it's weird, I do feel pretty good this morning. I've got a good feeling about the lottery. I think we're all going to sail through it. You should have more confidence. Maybe it's all that chanting Helen's been doing for me, but I feel okay.

"Anyway, bro. That was fun last night. Hey, I'm going to cook up some eggs and bacon. Come on up if you want. Or you can wait for Helen to wake up. But come up. We're going to need all our strength today, right?

"Thanks again, man. Later.

"Wait — you still there?

"Whatever happened to Jennifer last night, anyway?"

# 21.

# Jennifer

**H**elen woke up and asked, "Was that Charlie?"

"It's okay," I said. "He's fine. Not that it makes anything all right. But he's fine, Helen. He wants us to come up for breakfast."

I sat on the bed. She was still in it. The winter sunlight lit her. Her hair was strewn about the pillow. Her face was pink and her lips looked swollen. I didn't remember her lips being so full. Maybe I had never really looked at them in this way before. Maybe I'd never really seen her before. She was now someone new to me, and I knew that the grace of not caring about her was not mine to have.

"Oh God oh God oh God," she said.

"I know," I said.

"*You* know?" Helen said, not angrily. "*You're* not married. No. This is very bad for me."

She pulled the covers up around her. I put my hand on her shoulder, over the blankets and sheets. I didn't move my hand. I closed my eyes. This was Helen. This was Helen.

"Casey."

Her face was half covered by the blankets. "You have to know. This can never . . . ."

"Of course. Nobody. Only us. I would never."

"I mean *nobody*, Casey. Nobody. This never happened."

"Nobody, Helen."

I took my hand off her. I looked at the top of her hair, swirling down her neck and back onto the bed, and mentally kissed her hair. But I knew I could never even do that again. I could never even kiss her hair again.

Jennifer wouldn't come to the phone and Benjamin wouldn't help get her. I'd never met the guy but I didn't like him. I was pretty sure he felt the same about me.

"She's unavailable," was all the old man would say.

I called her three times. Jennifer couldn't have found out about Helen and me. But she wouldn't come to the phone.

I wanted her old man to yell at me, or tell me not to call. But he didn't. He stayed icy and officious, like he secretly enjoyed this.

Helen had gone home to Charlie. I couldn't fathom what we had done. I wanted the night with Helen to be gone. I needed to see Jennifer, to put life back in its place, however imperfect that place had been.

I went to wake up Hairball. I never knew anyone to sleep as hard as he did.

"Get up, Hairball."

Nothing.

"Hairball, get up, I can't explain, you have to go with me. Get up."

"Whathefugsup?"

"Go with me to Jennifer's."

"Whathefugfor?"

"Something's up."

"Whathefugsup?"

"She won't talk to me. I need to find out what's going on."

Hairball sat straight up. His eyes were crusted yellow and red slits. His hair was matted in many directions. He looked at me with a basic reptilian awareness and made a few strange sounds with his mouth. Then he said, "Would you?"

"Would I what?"

"Would you talk to you?"

"Oh, what now?"

"You don't know?" My throat tightened and my stomach cramped.

"What."

Hairball lay back down.

"She saw you and Helen."

Hairball told me the story.

Helen and I were loud. Our noises woke him up, and that was nearly impossible. After he woke up he got up to go to the bathroom. His room was next to mine. He walked out in the hallway as Jennifer was coming up the stairs. She spotted him and said that her grandmother had gotten sick and she had had to help Benjamin get her to the hospital. She had tried to call but every time someone picked up the phone the party was so loud that no one could hear her. She told Hairball that she'd stayed up all night and wanted to come over and surprise me.

Neither Jennifer nor Hairball had known what was happening at first. My door had been open a little because it had an old black metal latch instead of a doorknob, and a screw was missing. Unless you slipped a hook into an eye above the latch it wouldn't stay shut. Hairball said he moved to Jennifer to stop her but before he could she gave the door a little shove. He said Helen and I were having oral sex when Jennifer and he first saw us. Neither of them said a word, he said. Jennifer watched us for only a few seconds and turned and ran down the steps. Hairball followed her, tried to follow her out to her car, but she peeled out and disappeared.

"If I were you," Hairball said.

"If you were me you'd start drinking right now. No thanks."

"No." Hairball had that look on his face, that look that reminded you why you liked him. A look like he was the nicest guy in the world.

"I'd take a shower, get something to eat, go write some bullshit down in my diary, then go outside and chop wood or take a walk with my dog."

His smile was big and open.

"Your life is extremely fucked up right now, Casey," he said. "What you need to do is let Jennifer cool off. Let Helen be Charlie's wife. Then wait to see if your life will be that much worse in . . ." — he rolled over and squinted at his ancient General Electric clock radio — ". . . in exactly six hours and twenty-five minutes."

I'd forgotten. Draft lottery day was here. The short day was putting the sun through its quick winter dance and getting ready to cover the whole country with darkness.

# 22.

# Chance

**A** man goes to Las Vegas and throws some dice and the wrong numbers come up and he goes broke. A woman across the casino puts her money down on a number and wins the big pot. The sun shines on one couple's wedding. The rain falls on another couple's wedding. A child breathes the wrong air at the wrong time and dies of a virus a week later. A man gets on the wrong plane and it crashes and he dies. Another man breaks his toe the same morning and misses the plane and he lives.

On draft-lottery day a guy's birthday is drawn on the number 309. Another guy's birthday is drawn on number 155. A third guy's number is drawn on number 5. A fourth guy's number is drawn on 44. The fifth guy's number is drawn on number 252.

Two guys get their physical notices. Three guys go on living and watching the war from a million miles away.

One of the guys who get their physical notices takes his cigarette and lights the notice and burns it up. He gets a second notice; this time it's also a warning. He leaves the second notice, the warning, on the kitchen table until it becomes so full of mustard and beer and milk that it becomes unrecognizable and leaves ink stains on the white metal kitchen table. Someone finally throws it away. The guy never gets another letter. The government — some draft board clerk, some divine screw-up with more important things on his mind — forgets about him.

The other guy with the low number gets his physical notice and goes and gets his physical. He is classified 1-A. Two weeks later he is drafted.

The guy doesn't know what to do. He hates the war. He is afraid. He talks to people about what he should do. People say all kinds of things. They say he should go to Canada. They say he should fight for his country. They say he is crazy and a coward if he goes. They say he is crazy and a coward if he doesn't go. Some people say he will betray his country if he goes and other people say he will betray his country if he doesn't go. Nearly everyone says he should do the right thing.

People say all these things. Then one day, over coffee, or a beer, or on the telephone, or in a letter, or on their knees praying, or to themselves sitting by the river, they say, "Charlie Kerrigan's gone to Vietnam."

# 23.

# Oz

‸

February is a lousy month in northeastern Ohio. The damp chill is relentless, the sky is usually gray. The wind blows hard across Lake Erie from Canada. As a month, February offers nothing but the promise of March. March offers at least the promise of April, of birds, of the smell of wet earth and new life. February is a month to get through.

The Tank's trunk was full of drum hardware, cymbal stands, a drum seat, an old snare drum I was trying to sell. The spare tire in the trunk took up half the space. We couldn't get Charlie's duffel bag in it.

"Don't bother cleaning out the trunk," Charlie said.

We put his duffel bag in the back seat and Helen rode between Charlie and me in the front seat.

Charlie's flight was to take off at 6:30 on Sunday morning. We were to leave Little Meadow at 5:15. I had slept an hour or two at the most. Charlie and Helen looked as if they hadn't slept at all, with their red, puffy eyes and pallid complexions.

Charlie walked up the stairs to say goodbye to Hairball and

Phil. Phil didn't wake up because Charlie wanted to be quiet so as not to wake Wendy. Charlie told me to tell him goodbye and to keep playing his guitar so we could all play together in a band when he got home from Vietnam.

Hairball woke up instantly. He brushed the hair out of his eyes and said, "Keep that big ugly head down, buddy." He got out of bed, buck naked, and hugged Charlie. Then Hairball cried. I'll never forget it: Hairball, at five o'clock in the morning, hugging Charlie and crying. "Love you, man," he said.

Charlie said, "You too, man. Take it easy."

Hairball was sniffling when we left and had turned his record player on. The Grateful Dead.

We walked to Jeff's room downstairs. It was very cold in there and you could see your breath. Jeff slept with about six blankets.

"Hey Jeff," Charlie said. "I'm off. Take it easy." Jeff didn't wake up, either.

The three of us got out of the car at the airport and I got Charlie his duffel bag. We shook hands. I thought I might lose it and I felt vomit coming up from my stomach and held it in. Nothing seemed appropriate to say, so I said, "See you, Charlie." My chest hurt and I could hardly breathe.

Charlie's face broke into one of his rare smiles. "I think I'll miss you most of all, Scarecrow," he said.

"Charlie's a Wizard of Oz freak," Helen said without smiling. "That's a compliment, Casey." She looked awful.

"I'm off to see the Wizard," Charlie said. "I'm off to Oz."

I stayed in the car. There was an unspoken understanding among us that Helen and Charlie should be alone inside the airport.

I waited in the car for about a half hour until Helen came back. She looked as if God had picked her up and wrung her out like a rag. She got in the car and all I felt was emptiness.

"I wish it wasn't so sunny," Helen said on our way home from the airport. "It doesn't seem right that it's so sunny. Of all the days to be sunny. Of all the days to be sunny, huh?"

We drove the forty-five minutes home with the sun beating down on us and by the time we got back to Little Meadow Helen had fallen asleep. I pulled the car up her driveway and put it in Park.

Fifteen more minutes went by and Helen kept sleeping. I was tired, too, and let her sleep while I thought about Charlie and where he was going. After a while I turned in my seat and watched Helen sleeping. She was dressed in a brown-and-tan plaid skirt, brown blouse and tan suede boots. She wore a red parka. She had put on a little lipstick and eye shadow and her mascara was smudged from when she cried at the airport. Her parka was open and I could see that her stomach was starting to show her pregnancy.

The vibration from the car engine combined with the sun through the windshield and the warm air from the heater and made the car lulling and comfortable. She was completely out and I had nothing else to do for the whole day. I studied her face. Her mouth was wide and full; her nose strong and straight; her cheekbones high, leading to a smooth, curving jaw. I wanted so badly to hold her that I started feeling sick; then I thought about my best friend on a plane to Fort Dix in order to prepare to go to Vietnam and I thought there might not be a sicker thing for anybody to think about than what I was thinking about. It was at that moment when I came to know that I was completely in love with Helen.

# 24.

# Spring

If Hairball had any guilt over ignoring the notices to take his physical and blowing off the United States government, he didn't show it. But he worried about Charlie.

Charlie went to basic training at Fort Dix. The entire time he was there Hairball fretted that Charlie might kill himself.

"My brother knew a guy whose brother slit his wrists," Hairball said to me as we sat at Whirly's one Friday night. "They treat the recruits like dog shit, and Charlie isn't somebody who can put up with that. He's too cool for that bullshit, man."

But Charlie made it through Fort Dix. I heard from him once, when he called from a phone booth. He wanted to know how Helen was, how the guys were, how I was.

"I can't really talk now. You don't want to hear about this anyway. It's not exactly my scene," he said. He sounded nervous.

Helen said she got letters from him, but that they didn't say much. He hadn't gotten his orders yet but it was almost certain he would be shipping out for Vietnam soon.

She chanted with the Japanese ladies, went to Buddhist meetings. Yuki Osaki, the lady from the Buddhist meeting we had gone to that past fall, became her best friend. She was there every day, always wearing a nice dress, always smiling and laughing. I got to know her a little, and she was the only one I'd chant with. It gave me a little peace of mind. I remember thinking that Yuki might be a lady Buddha.

Every now and then Helen came over to the farmhouse. I'd make her tea and we'd talk about Charlie, the war, about the baby she carried. She'd rub her belly and say, "I felt a little kick," or "He's giving me fits lately," but she'd smile and I could tell she was excited about the baby. The baby was due in June.

We never mentioned the night of the party. I wanted to try and get it in some kind of perspective but it seemed like it would be a violation. I kept remembering her saying that night, "This never happened."

The guys were kind to Helen. Hairball made her laugh and liked to cook for her. He fed her liver and onions, or steak and baked potatoes, or anything he thought she needed to stay strong for, as Hairball said, "that little munchkin you got in there."

Phil sang to her, which she loved. He'd written a half-dozen songs about Wendy Winton, who by now was his near-constant companion when she wasn't attending art classes at Kent State. Phil would replace Wendy's name with Helen's, which worked well enough because they were both two syllables. Wendy never seemed to mind. As Charlie had predicted, she was good for Phil, and Phil seemed to blossom. For one thing, he stopped playing "Little Girl Sad." We liked Wendy if for no other reason than that.

Jeff chanted and went to Buddhist meetings. In front of his *But-*

*sudan* was a white 5 x 7 card that said, "Charlie." He talked with Helen in quiet tones about faith, about the need to send Charlie good fortune, about Charlie needing to fulfill his karma in Vietnam. He told her not to try and figure it out, that the reasons were beyond them but that Charlie's destiny could be changed for the better by other people chanting for him.

I don't know if Helen believed Jeff, or if she believed Yuki and the Japanese ladies, or if she believed in the power of chanting, or if she believed in anything. She always looked to me like she was in a mild state of shock. I saw her sadness and it overwhelmed me. All I could offer her was friendship, and she took it.

March. The Weather Underground sets off a bomb at the Capital Building in Washington. No injuries, but extensive damage. Laos is invaded. Heavy casualties, more than four hundred Americans killed. Vice President Spiro Agnew calls war protesters "homefront snipers."

April. Vietnam Veterans Against the War throw their old uniforms, helmets, medals and ribbons on the steps of the Capital in a surrealistic demonstration. They are met by five thousand police and twelve thousand troops.

In the middle of spring I called up Jennifer. I had called her a few times before but she would never come to the phone.

This time I called her on a Saturday afternoon. I'd been drumming with The Recliners in downtown Cleveland three times a week. I called her up to see if she wanted to go to my gig that night. She could hang out with me but we wouldn't have to talk.

She answered the phone.

"Jennifer hi this is me please don't hang up."

Silence, but at least she was still there.

"Can we get together and talk? Just talk?"

The gig idea suddenly seemed bad. I heard her sigh.

"You are such an *asshole.*"

"I am, I know."

"Did Charlie ever find out?"

"No."

"Well, I never told anybody."

"I know. Thanks."

"God, you're *such* an asshole."

"I know, Jennifer. I just want to talk to you. Can we go to Dink's for some tea or something? Like today, like now?"

"Why? What's there to say?"

"I don't know. I can fill you in on what's been going on."

"Like you filled Helen in?"

"Okay. Good one. Right. But I think we should meet."

"Tell me why?"

"Because we had a good thing. I don't know."

"Tell me why?"

"Because . . . what. What am I supposed to say?"

" *Tell me why I should meet you.* "

"Because I'm such an asshole? I don't know."

"That's right, as a matter of fact. Because you're such an asshole. And I'm going to meet you because I want to hear what you could possibly tell me about that night that could possibly change my opinion of you. Dink's, five o'clock. I'll drive myself."

She hung up.

It was warm so I walked to downtown Chestnut Falls. I sang

all the way. I felt pretty good for a change; I sensed maybe things were going to open up for me. I sang Beatles songs at the top of my lungs and thought about what the world should be like.

The Beatles would get back together, except that now Ringo would finally open that hair salon he'd been talking about because he was tired of playing drums. He never learned how to do a drum roll and decided to pack it in. The lads reluctantly said okay and good luck to Ringo. The remaining three decided to hold open auditions for drummers. I'd use the money I'd made drumming to fly to London for the audition. The Beatles would winnow it down to four drummers. I saw John and Paul talking about me after my audition.

"He's got sumthin', he does," John would say. "Sumthin' special."

"Hey then lad — can ya sing?" Paul would say.

That would be the clincher. I'd stun them with perfect harmonies on "This Boy," "If I Fell," and anything else they could throw at me. I even did a rousing rendition of Ringo's tune, "With A Little Help From My Friends."

George would chime in, "You're all bloody daft if you can't see he's bleedin' perfect for the band."

And that would be it: I'd be the Beatles' new drummer.

Charlie would get home from Vietnam on the same day the Beatles made their announcement from the Abbey Road Studios, where we were about to make our first post-Ringo album, entitled, "Get Back Together . . . Again."

I'd tell the lads that I wanted to fly my best mate over — after all, he just got back from Vietnam.

"He can play a track or two on the LP," George would say. "Sounds like your mate could use the gig, hey?"

"Give Charlie a chance, all right then, John?" Paul would say, and John, George and I would laugh heartily. Yoko would even crack a smile.

Helen would come with him. The minute she'd walk off the plane I'd realize that I loved her — but like a sister! Helen and I'd laugh and talk — Can you believe how crazy I acted? I'd say. But no matter, Charlie's back and everything is cool.

That's when Jennifer would show up at the studio door.

"Helen said you might be needing some company," she'd say in her unbearably charming way. She'd be wearing some sexy new threads from Carnaby Street. She'd have on this wild hat with fake blue feathers all over it.

"Nice lookin' bird. You fancy her, do you?" Paul would say with a grin as we played our first tune, "The Way of Jenny," written by none other than Philip Rosenbaum. Phil! I'd given John and Paul some of his tunes and they'd flipped. Phil was to be the new "fifth Beatle," contributing an occasional song and playing some lead guitar when George was touring solo. (George had insisted on keeping his solo projects alive.)

"I mean, she's not bad, is she then, Mac," I would say to Paul with a slight Liverpudlian sing-song inflection in my voice. I couldn't help it; what nineteen-year-old guy wouldn't like to talk like a Beatle for the right reason?

Paul would get a kick out of the fact that I'd called him "Mac." "Cheeky Yank, John, isn't he?" Paul would respond.

"Best kind," John would reply.

"Play the bleedin' tune, would you now," George would say to the new Beatles in mock disgust, then give me a wink.

By the time I got to downtown Chestnut Falls I was actually

quaking with excitement. It was springtime. I was playing with the Beatles. This was a *great* life.

I crossed Church Street, made my way to Franklin Street, and headed down to Dink's.

It was apparent from the start that Jennifer had no appreciation of me as a prospective Beatle.

"Hey, Jenny," I said and tried to kiss her.

"No way," she said, turning her head. "And don't call me Jenny. Let's sit down."

She ordered french fries and a Coke. I ordered the rice pudding and a glass of water.

"Why do you only drink water with that?" she said. She was irritated as hell with me.

"This is extra groovy rice pudding, Jenny," I said in a Beatles accent. "It's absolutely fab-gear, then, isn't it?"

"Sarcasm. That's good," she said. "That helps."

"I get obnoxious when I'm nervous. Been this way since elementary school."

We exchanged no further pleasantries. When your girlfriend has seen you having oral sex with your best friend's pregnant wife, pleasantries can be superfluous.

Finally: "I don't know what to say, Jennifer."

"Really."

"I don't know what happened that night."

"Really."

The rice pudding was perfect as usual, with burned skin on top and a tender, rice-filled middle. I ate for a while.

"That's it?" she said.

I put my spoon down. She was holding a french fry and kind of waving it up and down. She looked stunning. Her cheeks were red from the cold and she had on a black turtleneck, black jeans and a black sweater. Her clothes looked expensive. I wished I was wearing something other than jeans and an old gray sweatshirt with dirt stains on the wrists.

"It was a mistake."

"And Helen? How does she feel about the fact that you took advantage of her?"

"Wait a minute."

"No, you wait a minute, Casey. Hairball told me she was drunk and stoned. You fucking waited until Charlie was gone and you went after her. You're a piece of garbage, you know that?"

"Hairball said I attacked her?"

"No. Hairball only said everybody had been drinking. But you're a piece of garbage anyway."

"You sound mad."

"I'm not mad, darling. I'm just not your girlfriend anymore."

"Jennifer."

I felt trapped, like a criminal.

"It wasn't bad like that. Please don't do this."

"I'm with someone else now, Casey."

I put my head in my hands and waited for the explosion to detonate.

She waited a minute, ate a few french fries, drank some Coke.

"I'm with someone else now, anyway," she repeated.

"I wish you wouldn't do this. I really like you, Jennifer."

"I'm with a new young man now."

*A new young man*? What girl in my universe referred to anyone as "a new young man?"

"A new young man? Who is it?"

"Nobody you know. Benjamin knows him from the tennis club. He's the pro there. Kenneth Tomarsin. He's twenty-five and treats me really nice."

"*Kenneth*? Like Mr. Kenneth the hair dresser? He's a tennis pro and he goes by *Kenneth*? Is he . . . ."

I was going to say, "Is he a homo?" but Jennifer hated that kind of sophomoric humor and I kind of hated myself for feeling mean. Then Gilbert Blakely flashed across my mind, and I thought how Jennifer would probably rather be with a cool homosexual like Gilbert than "garbage" like me anyway, and so I stopped.

"Don't be a complete fool. You're digging a deeper hole."

"Listen Jennifer, there's something I need to tell you. This is a mistake."

"No it's not."

"Yes it is."

I looked up at the clock on the wall. Jennifer continued eating her french fries. The Beatles were broken up for good. Charlie was in Nam. The world seem to deflate as each second ticked by.

"I love you, Jennifer."

"Oh Casey, please. No you don't."

She was right. I didn't. But the phrase had been building up in me for so long that I had to say it to somebody.

And I was sure the woman I really wanted to say it to didn't want to hear it either.

# 25.

# Letter

June 11, 1971
Hue, Vietnam

Dear Casey,

Sorry I haven't written to you sooner. I had good intentions of writing you and the guys at Little Meadow but it hasn't worked out too well. I write Helen about once a week. That may seem like a lot, but some of the guys here write their wives every day if they can.

This letter is just for you to read because I want to say some things that are better left between us. I trust you not to tell Helen the heavy stuff. The letters I write to her are mostly bullshit, but I can't bring myself to tell her what this place is really like and what I think is going to happen to me.

I'm scared out of my mind most of the time. I'm so scared that it scares me. I had no idea how frightened a human being could get and still live. It seems like you would drop dead, being as afraid as I am.

No one, when it comes down to it, seems to understand this war.

*Even some of the guys who came over here gung-ho about killing commies get freaked out about it. Some of them are the worst off. Once they take that jump and realize they've been sold down the river, they lose it. They're the ones you have to worry about sticking you with a knife or running off into the jungle for good.*

*Actually, I did figure out how scared I am, at least I can take a stab at it. I thought this up one day on patrol. I'm as scared as much as I love Helen. That's as much as I can be — maximum. It's a bad combination — being this scared and this much in love.*

*I tell Helen I love her in my letters, but I don't tell her how much. I don't know why. Maybe because if I tell her how much I love her, I'd also tell her how scared I am. If this doesn't make sense, I'm sorry. I'm shaky a lot these days. I've always been kind of a shaky sort, you know? Well, you know. That's why I like to pound them down at Whirly's. You learn that kind of stuff about yourself over here.*

*Something really bad happened. Last week a kid named Arlen Anderson stepped on a booby trap and it blew him into so many pieces that he could only be identified by his dog tag. He was the best friend I had over here. It's not like I knew him that well, but he was an okay guy and we hung out.*

*We talked a lot about our wives — Arlen was only 20 but he had been married for a year. He worked at his dad's pet and garden center near Dayton, as a matter of fact.*

*The thing is about Arlen, the thing that I can't get out of my mind, except for when I sleep, is that I can't figure out why he died. I feel like writing his wife but I don't know what to tell her. What would you say? That Arlen died for his country? Who believes that anymore? Some people do. I don't. Arlen didn't. At least not at the end.*

*He was a sweet kid, as they say. He talked about how he wanted to have a cabin in the woods and write science fiction books and have a dog and a fireplace and his wife and kids and the whole thing. In that way he reminded me of you, kind of naive and idealistic. (No offense.) He even talked about what kind of dog he wanted. I told him about Lion and he said that Border Collies were fine but that he had to have an Old English Sheepdog like Paul McCartney's dog. He sang McCartney's song about his dog — "Martha My Dear." His voice sounded pretty good. I told him maybe he could sing in our band so he got excited and told everybody that he and I were forming a band when we got back to The World.*

*The day after he sang Martha My Dear Arlen and three other guys in his patrol walked into a NVA booby trap. The booby trap blew their body parts all over the place. I saw it — arms, legs, one guy's head. Oh, man, Casey. You don't want to know. It was beyond anything I could ever have thought about.*

*It's tough getting close to anyone over here. Not a good idea if you don't want to spend your time identifying your buddies' remains. It's still very hard for me to write about. Arms, legs, and a head. I think about that all the time — arms, legs and a head.*

*Last week, at about three o'clock in the morning, our base was shelled by the VC. It's a fairly regular thing. We're sleeping and suddenly there's artillery shells going off close by and they sound like they're in my bunker. Some of the guys go crazy and run around, but I tend to not move. I just wait to get hit. I don't know which is better. Soldiers seem to get killed either way. Anyway, on the night I'm talking about, a shell went off about 50 feet from my bunker. Usually we worry about the NVA, but in this case the VC had gotten through the perimeter — sometimes that happens and they harass us to drive us nuts — and they got maybe 6 or 7 shells into our camp. This one shell was the loudest thing I've ever heard, like having your head inside a bass drum and multiplying it by a thousand. It was so loud that I swear my bones had ears.*

*I couldn't hear a thing for four days. I was deaf. I mean, if some-one stood right in front of me and screamed and I watched their mouth it sounded like they were a couple hundred feet away. I still get a God-awful ringing in my ears, like a million crickets, except that they don't sound nice like at Little Meadow. It's bad. The ringing's enough to make you crazy.*

*Here's the part I don't want you to talk to Helen about. Casey, I think I'm going to get killed. I've never been very lucky, except for Helen. She may be the only luck I'll ever have. It's a bad thing, thinking you'll get killed. I know that, believe me. It's the worst thing you can do, to think like that. I should be more positive. But I can't shake the feeling, and it scares me, man. I don't like being scared, as you may know.*

*It's insane over here, more than we thought, no matter how much bad shit we heard before. I see guys freak out all the time. There's a guy in my company named Ray whose girlfriend broke up with him right after he got here. When he first got here he talked about her all the time, about how they were going to get married and how his parents and her parents were getting to know each other, and how they were getting married in a VFW Hall because her old man's a veteran of World War II, and his brother was going to throw him a bachelor party with strippers but that he wasn't going to bang any of them because it would hurt his fiancée if she found out. A lot of regular all-American stuff. Then he got the letter. She told him that she had thought about it, and that she couldn't really respect him because the war is wrong and that she was moving in with one of her professors from Purdue. Bro, you never saw anyone change like Ray did. He cried like a baby for two days, and then he got real steely. After that he was a regular killing machine. I haven't even seen a VC or* an NVA, much less killed one, but Ray has at least 10 kills to his credit. I heard that the VC have names for certain guys on our side, guys that are particularly deadly, and that Ray is one of them. He brags that the VC have a bounty on his head. It's real strange, because Ray painted a heart with a crack in it on his helmet and his ex-girlfriend's name. Her name is Laura. You can't imagine how strange it is. You see this baby-faced guy with a broken heart on his helmet and "LAURA" in block letters like a little kid would write. Then you hear that Ray got two more kills and you see him eating his C-rations and laughing and talking to anybody who'll listen about the kills. He talks about them like some old guy talks about his golf game: "First I hit a nice drive on that dog-leg left on number fifteen and then I chipped onto the green and two-putted." Ray will say, "I saw Charly in the elephant grass and the little bastard wasn't moving, so I kept him in my sights for five minutes until I knew that he knew he was safe. I watched his face relax and then he took out a handful of rice and just when he put it in his mouth I shot him in his face. Blew his fucking head right off."

Then he laughs like crazy. He laughs and laughs and gives guys the high-five and dances around.

It's a real pleasure to listen to Ray. Certainly it makes me feel like I understand the meaning of life. Hey, Case, why don't you go and sign up? I know you'd enjoy this.

Sorry, man. I get sarcastic, you know? I can't help it.

I have this tendency to divide everyone here into two types: guys who think they'll make it out alive and guys who don't. Also, guys who believe what we're doing here is right and guys who think it's either wrong that we're here or that there's no reason we're here. The guys who think we're doing good work for God and country think they'll make it back to the World. Those guys are tough, the ones like the Special Forces.

*Tough as nails, Case. I don't even talk to them. Nothing seems to bother them and that freaks me out.*

*The guys who don't think we should be here tend to believe that they'll die. Unfortunately, I'm one of those. One thing I can tell you is that it isn't by choice. I'm the way I am and there's nothing that can change it.*

*You're probably wondering why I haven't mentioned Sara. I don't know her. I've never met her. It's so hard to think about my baby girl that I try not to, not that it works very well. Watch out for her for me, will you? Oh, hell, that's a lousy thing to say to someone. But you know what I mean. Keep a weather eye out, okay? (Is that the phrase?) I want to see her more than I've ever wanted anything in my life. That's all I can say about it.*

*Some of the music we get to hear is pretty good, anyway. There's one new tune that's great and I'm a hundred per cent positive that you are into this song. It's called "Layla" by Eric Clapton's new group. Did I hear right and the band is called Derek's Dominoes or Derek and the Dominoes or something? Who else is in the band, I wonder. It's the best song I've heard in a while. We should do that one in our band. Damn, Clapton can play. The other song I like is "Power to the People" by John Lennon. I'm still bummed out that the Beatles broke up but I'm glad Lennon's putting out some good music. I've got it in my mind to try to write some songs. Maybe I could co-write something with Phil. Has he written anything new? I hope so. Sometimes I think about that song of his, "Little Girl Sad," and I laugh. Tell him thanks for that. I don't laugh about much. On second thought, don't say that. It would hurt his feelings.*

*Oh, I just had my 22nd birthday. Happy birthday to me. Throw back a Jack and a Stroh's at Whirly's for me. Then give Helen a kiss. On the cheek, you horny bastard.*

*Charlie*

# 26.

# Mystery

꩜

**H**umidity hung in the July air. A few birds sang lazily in the Ohio heat. In the meadow the foxglove, which had gone to seed weeks earlier, began to bloom, their upside-down violet-colored bells once again waving silently in the moist south breeze. The purple meadow sage came back in bloom after dimming and disappearing weeks before. Fat wild raspberries ripened on vines that grew along a rusted metal fence that ran between the Tudor house and the farmhouse and then stopped inexplicably.

Catherine Smith worked on her vegetable garden that grew at the far southern border of the Tudor house's property. Mrs. Smith lived in an apartment across town, but maintained a quarter-acre garden of tomatoes, cucumbers, radishes, onions, corn, and various herbs. "My Simon and Garfunkel garden," she called it, with its parsley, sage, rosemary, and thyme, as well as fennel and chive.

I arrived home from my landscaping job and saw Mrs. Smith walking around in her garden, checking out the radishes.

I greeted her and asked her if everything was all right.

"Fine, thank you, Casey," she said. "You?"

"Pretty good, thanks. We're all worried about Charlie."

"I'm sure he'll be fine. It's such a shame, though. This war's a terrible thing."

She took my hand in both of hers. I'd never known Mrs. Smith to offer a merely perfunctory handshake. She led me toward a medium-sized tree at the back of the property where the garden met the woods.

"Do you see this, Casey? It's the oddest thing," she said. She had soft, kind blue eyes and wavy red hair. She wore a blue-and-white cotton print dress. She was in her late forties. I loved the way she talked, like some actress in a black-and-white movie from the late thirties, with that refined, strong, almost English accent.

"What is it, Mrs. Smith?"

"This magnolia tree should have stopped blooming by mid-June, perhaps earlier. But it's blooming now. Smell."

I leaned down and put my nose to the creamy, eight-petaled blossom that sat squarely in the middle of a six-point leaf.

"Wow," I said. "That smells amazing, like honey and grapefruit and perfume."

"Isn't it wonderful?" she said, her eyes shining and narrowing in a smile. "I planted this tree when Mr. Smith was alive. He died in 1963, you know."

"Same year as President Kennedy," I said.

"Yes, same year," she said. "Now, when I smell these blossoms, I think of Jack. My husband's name was Jack, too."

"They sure smell good."

"Sometimes, Casey, this is all we have when people die. These things . . . ." She swept her hand across the meadow's vista. "These things that grow — this meadow, this tree, these flowers."

"They die too," I said.

"They come back, or something in their place does," she said.

"People don't come back. Unless you believe the Buddhists."

She cupped a magnolia blossom in her hand and smelled it again and smiled.

"But they do, Casey," she said. "Jack — my husband — just did. When I smell these blossoms, he comes back to me."

Mrs. Smith looked out again over the meadow. She pointed to a colony of dame's rockets. Two tiger swallowtail butterflies flew around the light red flowers.

"Look at that," she said. "How exquisite, Casey. If that isn't the mind of God, I don't know what is. You can learn everything you need to know about life right here."

"There's a lot I don't know. I don't know much at all," I said. "There's a lot I don't understand."

"That's good," she said. "The most important thing you'll ever know is knowing what you don't understand, if that makes sense. Accepting the mystery of it all."

A cooling breeze blew in from the northwest. The meadow moved and made whispering sounds. The sun was low and pleasantly warm. I didn't know what to say so I stood there and watched her while she gardened. She was on her hands and knees and hummed something in a light voice. I thought about my family, that I loved them and that it was strange to be alive and have a family and be standing and watching Mrs. Smith do her gardening. I thought about not understanding anything.

I didn't offer to help her. I just stood there. It was the first time I'd felt all right about life in a long time.

# 27.

# Summer

꘎

I was lying on my balcony. It rained so hard earlier that my boss called it a day and let us go home. Now the steam rose in the meadow as the sun burned away the rain. I was sleeping the kind of perfect day-time sleep you have when you leave the work world and you have nothing to do but put your face up to the sun and drift off.

I heard the crunch of gravel across the meadow. A black Chevrolet Impala was being driven slowly up Helen's driveway. Gravel dust trailed behind the big car. It was four-ten in the afternoon.

Something looked weird about the car. It didn't have police markings on it but it seemed dull and official. Not like a car anybody cared about. Not even like a beater that somebody liked running down, caring about it in some perverse way, caring about messing around in it and wrecking it.

Adrenaline shot through me. I was in my underwear, still full of grass and gasoline and sweat. I jumped up, ran into my bedroom and found my jeans and Birks. My face and hands were dirty but I ran down the stairs and out the side-porch door. I ran as fast as I could across the meadow.

As I got closer to Helen and Charlie's house I began to fear the black Chevrolet and the man in the green uniform and green hat who got out of the car and walked toward Helen's door. Everything he wore looked too hot to wear under the broiling sun.

Terror bubbled up through my blood and flooded my brain; I wanted to suck time backwards.

The man in the green army uniform moved toward Helen's door just as I moved toward him.

He knocked on the door.

"Hey," I yelled out to him and walked faster. I couldn't run anymore because my breathing had become short.

"Hey!" I yelled again to him.

"*Nam-myoho-renge-kyo,*" I said a few times. Then, "Dear Jesus Lord in heaven please don't let Charlie be dead." I felt crazy. My heart pounded so hard I thought it would explode. I wanted to grab on to something.

Helen came to the door. I was maybe thirty yards away. I was breathing heavily.

I kept walking until I got to the line of white pines that separated the farmhouse property from Helen's house. There was a strip of grass about eight feet wide and then a gravel driveway. I stopped in the middle of the driveway, no more than ten feet from Helen and the man in the green uniform and formal hat.

I missed the first words of their conversation but he must have introduced himself and made sure she was Mrs. Charlie Kerrigan.

By the time I could hear him he said, "Mrs. Kerrigan, on behalf of the armed forces of the United States of America and the United States Army I have the sad duty to inform you that your husband,

Private First Class Charles Michael Kerrigan, was killed while in the service of his country, in Hue, Vietnam, on twenty-six July, nineteen seventy-one. On behalf of the President of The United States and the United States Army, please accept our deepest condolences for your loss."

The man in the green uniform and hat did not sweat. He looked calm and depressed. He looked like a man who felt bad but could do nothing about it.

I hardly recognized Helen. Her face looked like a thin gray gauze had come down over it. She didn't blink. She reminded me of a wax statue.

"Is there anything I can do for you, ma'am?" the man said. "Notify any relatives, Private Kerrigan's immediate family? The army can help you with burial arrangements if you need. I'm sorry to have to bring this up at this time, Mrs. Kerrigan, but the army will need your signature and permission to deliver the body to the place of burial or cremation. Private Kerrigan, of course, is entitled to a military funeral, but you don't have to decide on that right now."

The man in the green uniform waited for a half a minute. For all I could see, Helen didn't move or say anything. She closed her eyes. Lion left me and trotted over to the door, past the man and into Helen's house. Helen opened her eyes and reached down with her left hand and touched Lion as he walked inside.

"Here's a telephone number, Mrs. Kerrigan," the man said. "These people will help you through your difficult time. With burial arrangements, relative notification and such. I urge you call them, ma'am. I believe you'll find them very helpful."

The man took off his hat and fingered the brim, turning it in his hands a few times. Then he put it back on. Helen didn't see him do it because she kept her eyes closed.

"On a personal note, Mrs. Kerrigan, I'd like to say that it is my understanding that Private Kerrigan was a good soldier and spoke of you often. It is a shame to lose a fine young man like him, ma'am, but for what it's worth, his country is very proud of him. I'm sure you are, too."

Helen finally opened her eyes. I thought she might say something angry, lash out at the man in the green uniform. I was ready to break it up if she hit him.

"Thank you," she said.

I don't think she could even see him, or anything at all. I kept expecting her to cry but she didn't. She just looked straight ahead.

Lion walked back out the door and lay right at Helen's feet and looked over at me and made one of his big dog sighs. My lips had gone numb and I thought I might float away. The man just kept standing there.

Helen closed the door softly. The man in the green uniform walked back toward his black Chevrolet sedan. As he was getting into his car he looked at me.

"Charles Kerrigan a friend of yours?" he said.

"Charlie. Yes."

He looked back toward Helen's house.

"Nice young woman, Mrs. Kerrigan," he said.

"She's a widow now," I said.

"Unfortunately she is," the man said. He got in his car.

He backed his car part of the way down the driveway, then stopped, slid over on the maroon vinyl seat and rolled down the passenger window, which faced me.

"I'm sorry about your friend," he said.

He sat for a few seconds and looked at Helen's door.

"Can you imagine having my job?" he said.

"Hey look," I said. "How did he die? I mean, how did Charlie get killed?"

"Private Kerrigan caught a piece of shrapnel in the neck during a mine explosion. I'm supposed to tell Mrs. Kerrigan that but I didn't think it would be a good idea."

"I'll tell her."

"That's up to you. I didn't want to."

"Did he live long? After he got hit?" I listened to my own voice like it was someone else's.

"Not long. A little while."

"Did he say anything?"

"He wasn't conscious, son. No."

"I have to ask you: Did you really know Charlie? I mean that part about him having been a good soldier and talking about Helen all the time. How would you know those things?"

"Do yourself a favor," he said. "Don't go. Don't tell anybody I told you this. But whatever you do, don't go. There's nothing left to do over there except get the hell out. Four years ago I would've told you to sign up and do your duty. But now . . . ."

He turned his head away from me and stared at Helen's door for about a minute. The cicadas were crazy loud and I heard a bullfrog from the pond begin his nightly courting. It felt like life had come to a stop and all that was left in the world were these animal languages I didn't know. Even the meadow seemed unfamiliar, hostile.

Finally, the man in the green army suit, who had taken off his formal green army hat and laid it on the seat next to him, opened the driver's door, turned around and looked down the driveway. Then he backed his black Chevrolet Impala sedan down to the street and drove slowly away.

# 28

# Hairball

❧

Chestnut Falls Cemetery smelled alive with vegetation: the tawny fields that bordered it with their hay-like smell of dried grass; the dusty scent of ironweed and goldenrod; the rich pine tree sap; the musky dampness under the perpetual shade trees; the sour overgrowth of vines; the early aster giving the air the scent of spice. There were the old tombstones at the cemetery, with their wind and rain-smoothed corners, their Anglo names and biblical passages etched not for eternity, but for a few hundred more years, until the last storm or layer of ice finally removes any worldly memory. Oak, maple, chestnut, hickory, elm, beech, dogwood and birch trees mixed with spruce, pine and fur trees. Many of the oldest and most spectacular trees in Chestnut Falls began growing there when Chestnut Falls wasn't Chestnut Falls. The cemetery wasn't big. It was a pretty, small-town cemetery, and it was where we buried Charlie Kerrigan.

Helen didn't want a military funeral. She said Charlie wouldn't have wanted it. I didn't know about that; if I had been Charlie I think I'd have wanted one. I wanted to tell Helen it might have been something guys like Charlie and me hated but wanted, but I don't think I could have explained it. I can't now.

The funeral was short. Helen's parents had flown in from Connecticut. Her older sister was out of the country, working in the Peace Corps, and couldn't get a flight home. Helen's dad seemed friendly and comfortable in his skin. He talked to me for a long time. We talked about Charlie some, but more about the Cleveland Browns. He was a New York Giants fan, an east coast guy with a sun-tanned face with crinkles around his eyes. He seemed very sure of himself. Whether he was I'll never know. He was an Episcopalian and made the comment, "The Lord works in mysterious ways," but I didn't get the impression he believed in the Lord one way or the other. He seemed like he'd rather sip on a gin and tonic and watch the Giants in his rec room than go to church. He might as well have been from Rome or Kyoto or Nairobi, as removed from my world as he was.

I watched him take care of Helen. He wasn't overbearing or cloying. He loved her a lot, you could tell, but he let her be as strong as she could be, and then as soon as she began to wilt, he'd put his arm around her and brace her. I admired him for that, enough that I decided not to ask him what he thought about the war. I didn't want to know.

What surprised me most at Charlie's funeral was who came. Of course, Jeff, Hairball and Phil came with girlfriends and siblings and parents. Hugo and Rondo and Johnny Kenston and his dad and a few others from The Camp came, but that didn't surprise me. Dave Staples and his mother came, and Gilbert Blakely showed up with his boyfriend. They all helped ease Helen's suffering for a couple of hours and none of them surprised me by being there.

Ernie Whirly showing up surprised me. What shocked me was that Whirly stood there with a bad, light blue polyester short-sleeved shirt and two cigars in his front pocket and black pants with polyester fuzz balls hanging off the seams, and Ernie Whirly cried like a baby from the beginning of the funeral to the end. That's mostly what I remember of the funeral. Ernie Whirly holding on to his wife and sobbing like it was the end of the world.

Hairball's bed was incredibly comfortable. It sank down almost to the box spring when you lay down on it. His room smelled like pot and soap and dust.

He sat in a corner and played records and I lay on his bed. The funeral had been earlier that day. Helen and her parents had gone off to a nice restaurant where her dad had made reservations. I told him about it at the reception at Charlie and Helen's after the funeral. I was flattered when he'd said, "You seem like a man who knows his way around — tell me where to take Helen and Sara and her mom after this."

I wanted to impress her old man so I told him to take everybody to the Raintree, the fancy new place in downtown Chestnut Falls.

"You know what you should have told him when he said you knew your way around?" Hairball said.

I was lying face down. Hairball's thin pillow smelled like stale beer. I didn't answer.

"You should have told him, 'You'd be surprised how much I know my way around your daughter.'"

"Jesus, Hairball," I said into the pillow.

"Hey man, you better lighten up about it. Charlie never found out. He died thinking of you as his best friend."

"I was his . . . ." I said and stopped.

"I know, I know," Hairball said. "You know what I mean."

I thought about Ernie Whirly crying at Charlie's funeral. Then I thought about Hugo almost getting his head blown off and how Mr. Kenston had shot that poor son of a bitch Isaac Hoskins and killed him and I thought about his eyes being so scared-looking even after he died.

I thought about Sara, Charlie's baby who would never have her father. I thought about how I had a high number and he had a low number and how crazy it all was, and now Charlie was dead and I was lying on Hairball's bed, healthy, all in one piece. I thought about Helen, and how no matter what I did I couldn't stop being in love with her, no matter what I told myself or how guilty I felt, I couldn't stop saying *I love you, Helen*, over and over again in my mind.

I felt dizzy and grabbed on to Hairball's bed. He said something about Charlie meeting up with Jim Morrison, Keith Moon, Jimi Hendrix and Brian Jones and forming a band in heaven.

My stomach did flip-flops and I felt like I was falling. I raised my head up and the room was spinning.

"Personally, I have very little doubt that there's sex in heaven," Hairball said. "If I know Charlie, he's jamming with his new band and porking Janis Joplin. I wish I could've porked Janis before she died."

A hurricane swirled in my head. I couldn't talk. Hairball sucked the pot smoke into his lungs and held it.

"You got to look at the bright side, man," he said, still holding

the smoke in. "I mean, what if that was true. That Charlie's . . ." —
what was left of the smoke that hadn't entered his lungs and blood
stream and brain blew out his mouth like a sudden warm gust of
wind — "getting laid and playing guitar and stuff."

I thought I was going to laugh but instead I began to cry. It
wasn't like any cry I'd experienced before. It was a cry that didn't
seem to come from me, but came to me, from somewhere new, an
alien place, an older place, from somewhere deep in the ocean,
maybe. The cry attacked me and I gave in, surrendered easily. I
cried for a long time, so long that Hairball got worried and left his
room and called up his mother and asked her how you could tell if
someone was having a nervous breakdown. He came back to the
room and asked me what my name was, what day it was, basic questions about my family and my job. He was very serious and kept
coughing nervously and he talked in an almost inaudibly low pitch.

I was face down on his pillow when I finally stopped crying. His
room was darker and that comforted me. I felt as light and clear as
water. My feelings were nearly gone and that felt good. I sat up.
Hairball looked terrified.

"You look like a monster. Boy."

"Sorry."

"Like a monster. Don't look at yourself yet. I was getting a little worried about you there. Boy."

"My life's not so great. I'm not, I don't know. I'm not anything,
I don't think," I said.

"At least we're alive, man," he said.

Somebody knocked at his door.

"Yes'm," he called out and coughed.

Phil opened the door. Wendy stood next to him.

Phil looked at both of us but seemed not to notice my red eyes and swollen face.

"It's probably not a great time to bring this up, but do you guys mind if Wendola here crashes with me for a while? I mean, crashes here? At Little Meadow? She digs it."

"I'll help out," she said. "I could even help Helen with Sara."

Hairball and I looked at each other. You couldn't help but like Wendy. I remember thinking, *Where do these people come from?* I meant these nice people, these good people like Wendy. They were out there in the warring world. I nodded at Hairball.

"Knock yourself out, you rascals," Hairball said. "Try not to break anything."

"What it *is*," Phil said in a soul accent and shut the door. Phil's door slammed a moment later. Hendrix played "The Wind Cries Mary," and soon the house was filled with the sounds of young love.

Hairball lit up another joint.

"I wish I could smoke that stuff," I said.

"You're probably better off," he said. I was unconvinced.

"Hey, Hairball," I said. I had put my face back down on his pillow.

"I know this is a terrible thing to say, man. I know this is bad and Jeff would probably say I'll get *botsu* for it but I've got to tell somebody."

"Fire away, Cap'n," Hairball said. "Can't be that bad."

"I'll never love anyone but Helen. I'll never get over her," I said. "It feels sick. I feel sick. It's a nightmare to feel this way. Especially now. After Charlie."

Hairball was silent for a while. He was thinking so hard I could feel it like air pressure.

"You'll get over her," he said. "But you know what, Case? If you never do, at least you'll know what love feels like. And that's good. You know, man?"

I didn't answer him. He moved around his room for a few minutes looking for something. His door closed and I cried again, this time quietly and this time it came from inside me, from a more familiar place, a childhood place. I fell asleep and slept hard and dreamless until the next morning. When I walked downstairs to make tea, Hairball was sleeping on the couch.

# 29.

# Meadows

❧

**P**hil, Hairball and Jeff struggled with Helen's mustard-colored couch. They tried to wedge it into the red-and-white U-Haul van that sat in Helen's driveway.

I held Sara and walked with Helen to the middle of the north meadow.

Helen looked south, toward the river.

"Don't forget to put out a salt lick for the deer this winter," she said. "They're used to it by now. They'll come looking for it."

A woodpecker pounded at a tree. Thick clouds covered the sun. I thought how much Sara looked like Helen, how peaceful she was.

We sat on soft, tall grass that had fallen over from its own weight. I began to put Sara in Helen's lap.

"She likes you, Casey. Let her sit with you."

Sara played with my fingers as Helen wove a necklace out of the long grass. When she finished, Helen placed it around Sara's neck. Oblivious to the gift from her mother, Sara slept.

Helen said, "Charlie cared about you. More than you knew.

He thinks . . . ." She shut her eyes and she aged in front of me. Grief radiated off of her. Tears squeezed out of the corners of her eyes and I just sat there. There was nothing I could do except wait for her to come back from the unfathomably sad place people go when someone they love has died.

I listened to my housemates talking and laughing. Their laughter blended with the murmuring Chestnut River that had swelled from late-summer thunderstorms. Finally Helen spoke again.

"He thought you were troubled. Maybe that's why he cared about you. He was so troubled himself."

I watched her breathe slowly and steadily, her long fingers weaving another necklace of drying grass.

"But he liked that. He once told me that people who aren't troubled in these times are the most troubled."

I played with Sara's toes as she slept. Charlie never saw her toes or her fingers. He never saw that she looked like Helen.

She paused, took a deep breath, exhaled slowly.

"Charlie didn't believe he would go to Vietnam. Not until right before he went. I don't know if he even believed it then.

"When you said you might go, Charlie knew — he believed — you wouldn't go. 'Casey couldn't go over there. Casey couldn't handle it.' That's what he said.

"I don't know if he was right about you," she said, tearing the necklace into small pieces and arranging them in a design on her jeans. "But I know that he couldn't handle it. That's what killed him."

We heard the sound of Helen's wooden kitchen table hitting the garage door.

"You're gonna break it in half, you maniac," Hairball yelled at Phil.

Jeff, who had been strumming a broom and singing, smacked Hairball on the back of the legs with it. Hairball ignored him.

"I try to think of something good that's come out of this," Helen said, stroking Sara's sparse, feathery brown hair. "But I can't think of anything. Nothing at all. Maybe you can. Charlie would say that if anyone could, you could. But I can't."

Phil stood on top of the van and sang an intentionally off-key version of a new hit song called "American Pie" while Hairball and Jeff threw fallen apples from the apple tree at him.

"It's as if we've been overcome by evil. They send off people like Charlie to war."

She looked at Sara.

"All those children over there. Babies, like Sara. So much death. They wanted Charlie to fight those people. For what, Casey? For what? I've lost my husband. Mothers lose children. Children lose parents."

An apple hit the van and made a ridiculous, playful thudding sound, making the guys roar with laughter.

"Do you know what Charlie wanted more than anything when he came back from Vietnam? Just to be *happy*. That's all. He didn't really care about any particular kind of work, or whether he played in a band or not, or if we had any money. He just wanted to feel happy.

"Sometimes, especially after we found out I was pregnant with Sara, Charlie would have these moments. He'd look so expansive, a sort of grand old man at twenty-one. When he would get like that, I would see him as an old man."

Helen brushed the tiny pieces of grass off her jeans, folded her hands in her lap, straightened her back and looked at me.

"I saw him as an old man, even when I met him. Maybe that's

why I married him. I imagined us growing old together."

Streaks of silver ran through Helen's hair in more places now. She had become noticeably grayer since Charlie had died. She'd become more beautiful to me. Even the deep circles under her eyes added to her beauty. I wanted to hold her. I didn't know if I wanted to comfort her or just wanted her, couldn't decide if holding her would be perverse or kind. Charlie was dead, but I was alive and I wanted to touch her face, draw her near.

Sara woke up, opened her eyes slowly, brought her tiny fists to them and rubbed. Helen held out her hands.

"I'll take her now, Casey."

Helen lifted up her red and black flannel shirt and gave her left breast to Sara. I locked my eyes on the U-Haul and watched as Hairball and Phil convulsed in laughter. Phil had come down from the roof of the van and Jeff lifted his tee shirt over his head and did a headless dance.

Helen looked down at Sara, then up at me.

"That's the difference between you and me, Casey. You'll spend the rest of your life trying to be happy. Like Charlie. You'll try to find meaning. You'll try to find hope.

"I won't do that. I'm going to live minute by minute. I'll raise Sara to be strong. I want her to have hope. I want her to try and be happy. But she won't know what I know. She won't know, at least while she's young, that evil conquered her father and killed him, and took him from her and from me."

I took my blue bandanna out of my pocket and gave it to Helen. "Use this."

She wiped her eyes and blew her nose and then laughed gently.

"I don't suppose you want this back."

She looked at me with wet eyes. My chest tightened. Could I tell my friend's widow that I thought I loved her? That now I wanted to be there for her? That I wanted her to feel hope again? I wanted to get up and run over to my three friends who were now lying on their backs, talking about something. Probably music. Certainly not Vietnam.

"That's the best I can do," Helen said. "To help my daughter have those things. I'll never have them. Not after what's happened to Charlie. Not after what's happened to me. I accept that."

She smiled. The circles under her eyes filled in with blood and she looked young again.

"You stay hopeful for Charlie, Casey. Try to be happy. When you don't want to be happy anymore, when you're older, when you find out how bad things can be — be happy for Charlie, if not for yourself. He never got the chance to be old. To lose hope and then try and get it back: he'll never have that luxury."

I looked at Helen nursing Sara. Helen never stopped hurting. She would have moments of pleasure and moments of joy, but the pain would become as unnoticeable as her blood.

"Sara won't even be thirty in the year 2000," I said.

"Helen drew her eyebrows together. "I'm sorry?" she said.

"I was just thinking. In the year 2000, Sara will only be twenty-nine years old."

Helen stroked Sara's ear. "The year 2000 sounds so far away. Modern. Cold."

"What I mean is that maybe by then there won't be any more war. I mean, you would think that war would be gone, wouldn't you? Sara can have a good life. You can have a good life too, Helen. Charlie would want that, right?"

She spoke in a whisper. "He would. Thank you."

The clouds had broken apart and that moment came when the sun is about to shine. Then it shone, and I could swear it shone on Helen and Sara first, before me, before it lit up anything else in the meadow.

"The sun . . . ." I said.

"What? The sun?"

"No, nothing."

"What. Please tell me. The sun?"

"The sun shone on you and Sara first. I mean, it lit you up. Like that night last year."

"Last year?"

"There was a light. On you and Charlie. At least it seemed like a light shone on you and Charlie. I think about it. I don't know. Just now it was like that, with the sunlight. A light shines on you sometimes, Helen.

"You're so beautiful, like an angel or something. I'm ridiculous, I know, but I think of you that way."

"Even after what happened? The night of the party? We were so bad, Casey. Some angel. You just idealize me."

"I know, I know. Charlie would say I'm a goofball."

"No he wouldn't. He'd say you're idealizing me."

"Some idealist. It's just that I think there's something more. I don't know what. But I don't want you to miss it, even after all this, Helen."

The crickets and cicadas began their sleighbell chanting, beckoning autumn.

"Promise me one thing, Casey."

Lion chased Hairball around the U-Haul and I could hear

Hairball wheezing and coughing and laughing.

"Promise me you'll try to make something of this."

"Of what?"

"Of this. Me, Sara, Charlie dying. Little Meadow. Us — even the night we were bad. Everything."

"How?"

"You'll think of something. Some day."

"I wish you weren't going, Helen. I wish you and Sara would stay at Little Meadow."

"Promise me you'll make something of this. You'll know when the time is right."

"I promise."

"Okay," she said, standing up. "We'll just go on. Who knows what could have happened, what life could have been? We'll never know. Sara and I will just go on. But you'll do that one thing. You'll make something of this."

I had no strength. I wanted to lie on the ground, go into the earth where it was cool and dark, where there was no threat of sunshine lighting Helen, where I wouldn't have to watch her leave.

"Do you know what you're going to do?" she said looking down at me.

"About what?"

"Your life, Casey. You can't walk around in the woods with Lion forever."

"I don't see why not," I said. I stood up.

"But you can't. Life isn't like that. You need to go off and challenge yourself. The war will end. Things will return to normal. Find something you like. Play music, write, do whatever you like to do."

"I already do those things," I said.

"Not really," she said. "You have to engage, Casey, go in, go under. You're skating on the surface. You have to live. You know? Find someone to love. Live."

Helen leaned toward me. "Kiss me now, Casey."

She kissed me on the lips. I put my hands on her waist and barely moved my fingers in an imperceptible caress. She closed her eyes.

"I'll always love you, Casey," she said, putting her head on my shoulder. I felt her cool face through my shirt. I knew she felt my heart beating. I inhaled and took in her scent of shampoo that smelled like pine. I touched her ear and kissed her forehead.

"I love you, Helen."

She mussed up my hair and pulled back. I kept my hands on her waist.

My hands fell to my side. I felt my spirit hollow out, as if some-one took a shovel and scooped the dirt out, preparing a space.

"The boys must be finished," she said. "I guess we're loaded up."

Helen smiled at me and my heart broke open. Waves of sorrow and joy rushed into the empty places and washed up over the shores of my life, lapping against my greed, my coarseness, my desires.

"We're ready to go," she said.

The U-Haul van sat in the gravel driveway. Hairball, Phil and Jeff were nowhere to be seen. Music from the farmhouse floated across the meadow. I heard voices singing along with the record player — harsh voices, sweet voices, young voices.

Helen held Sara and turned toward the U-Haul and the Tudor house that looked so old in the long shadows of the late summer afternoon. She walked away through the tall grass, her life rolling out before her like a green and endless meadow, mercifully forgiving, seeded with hope, as love fell upon her like rain.